WANTED: A WIFE FOR THE SHEIKH

DESERT KINGS, BOOK 1

DIANA FRASER

BAY BOOKS

Wanted: A Wife for the Sheikh
by Diana Fraser

© 2016 Diana Fraser
Print Edition
ISBN 978-1927323298

Crown Prince Malek of Sumaira needs the respectability of a wife—fast. Or at least his country does. And his new PA is happy to help him find one. After looking after her sick mother for years, the last thing Sophie wants is to be tied down. But will the idea of being tied down by this Michael Fassbender clone become an obsession she needs to get out of her system before it's too late.

—Desert Kings—
Wanted: A Wife for the Sheikh
The Sheikh's Bargain Bride
The Sheikh's Lost Lover
Awakened by the Sheikh
Claimed by the Sheikh
Wanted: A Baby by the Sheikh

For more information about this author, visit:
http://www.dianafraser.net

To my mum

CHAPTER 1

*P*aris in spring—it was so romantic, so beautiful. Sophie Brown sighed and gazed through the floor to ceiling windows at the fashionable people walking leisurely along the Champs-Élysées, bathed in spring sunshine. The sidewalks were lined with freshly leaved plane trees and, if she pressed her nose to the glass, she could see the Arc de Triomphe, a pale gray against the bright blue sky.

"Sophie!"

Sophie jumped away from the window and found herself face to face with her boss—Monsieur Claude, the hotel manager. He came closer and looked around with a supercilious smile, making sure no guest were close by. "I don't employ you to gaze out the window."

"No, sorry, I—"

"I don't want to hear any excuses. What is it with you lot today? My senior technician has gone AWOL and my kitchen staff spends more time looking out the window than working." Exasperated, he sighed. "Finish clearing away these cups and then stay in the kitchens for the rest of the day."

"Yes, sir."

She gave the table a quick wipe and was about to follow Monsieur Claude into the kitchens when he stopped suddenly. The hotel doors swept open and all eyes turned to a tall, dark man wearing an expensively cut black designer suit, who walked with purpose across the hotel foyer, looking neither right nor left. A phalanx of officials followed him, their white robes gleaming under the brilliant light cast by the gold and crystal chandeliers.

"Who is *that?*" Sophie muttered.

Claude glanced at her. "No one, to *you*. Get that tray into the kitchen, right away."

"Yes, sir." But she continued to gaze after the stranger. Whoever he was, with his athletic physique, perfect, spare bone structure, and piercing blue eyes, he exuded power.

"Sophie!" She turned to see Monsieur Claude, red-faced with anger. "If you spent as much time doing your job as you do gaping at our guests or out the windows, I'd be pleased with your progress. But, guess what? I'm not. If I catch you again, you're out. Now get back to work!"

Sophie pushed open the door to the kitchen, and began unloading her tray. *Damn!* She wanted this job. She needed a change from her former career in IT and this casual work suited her down to the ground—no ties, no responsibilities— just a few months work here, a few there, and move on again. After six years of being virtually housebound, caring for her sick mother, now gone, she was determined to see the world. The best way to deal with grief was to keep busy. Keep moving. And she would. She'd do whatever it took, she thought grimly, as she loaded the dishwasher with the dirty crockery.

CROWN PRINCE MALEK IBN AL-ABDULLAH of Sumaira checked his watch—half an hour until showtime. Half an hour until the meeting began and he had to give the performance of his life. The future of his country depended on him gaining the support of the other Desert Kings—the leaders of four kingdoms bound by geography and culture. But that was where the similarities ended. His own country, Sumaira, was by far the largest *and* the most vulnerable.

The meeting was an attempt to forge closer links between their countries. There would be strength in that unity—strength to withstand the relentless political, economic, and military threat from the great countries that bordered them.

They had a long agenda to get through but there was one item which wasn't on the agenda, one item that, he knew, was on everyone's minds—would he, after he was crowned King of Sumaira, be able to retain control of his once-great country, keep it strong against the ever-present external threat from the east?

He checked his watch again and walked up behind his executive assistant, Maryam, who looked up anxiously at his approach. The woman had been his father's EA for which only basic computer skills had been required, and those skills were being tested at this very moment.

Efficiency had not mattered to his father who was a suitable emblem for his country—large, charismatic, argumentative, and totally dysfunctional. Computer systems, diplomacy, strategy—none of it meant anything to his father. He'd ruled by sheer force of personality, leaving an unholy mess when he died. A mess which his EA certainly wasn't capable of sorting out.

She'd been able to hide her inexperience while at home, with help from colleagues, and a smooth, confident approach. But now, as she was forced to handle problems herself, her lack of skills was apparent. And, it appeared, his other advisers had limited computer skills. He was the most knowledgeable of the group—and that wasn't saying much.

She looked up at him now with terrified eyes. But they didn't soften him, only angered him. She was a symptom of everything that was wrong with his life. Flustered, she jiggled the mouse around, peered at the blank screen, and returned to tapping the keyboard.

With hands on hips, Malek stood looking expectantly at the empty screen. But it continued to be blank. "Maryam! Bring the presentation up. I wish to check it once more before we begin."

"Your Highness..." She furrowed her lovely brow. "I'm trying. But..."

"But?" he roared. "There must be no 'buts'. What's the problem?"

"I can't seem to find it."

"What?" He looked over her shoulder. "We updated it last night."

"I know... It's just..."

"Just what?"

"It's not there."

"Ridiculous! Let me look!" But after he made a basic search he could see that there was no version of his presentation dated the previous day. He stood and paced across the room, trying to contain the livid anger that suddenly filled him at his EA's incompetence. "You!" He pointed to one of his staff who was unsuccessfully trying to make himself invisible. "Get the hotel IT technician. Get someone. *Anyone* who can sort this out." The man appeared frozen to the spot. "Now!" Then he turned to his EA who had returned to her seat at the computer and was tentatively pressing random keys.

"What the hell has happened to it?"

"I think, I think... I must have deleted it."

"You what?"

Maryam was close to tears. "You kept saying I should keep things tidier on my computer, be more efficient so…"

"So you decided to delete the presentation I'm going to give in, let's see"—he glanced at his watch—"twenty minutes?"

"It was an accident."

Blood roared in his veins. He thrust his fingers through his closely cropped hair and twisted away. It wouldn't do any good to vent his anger on this woman. She was out of her depth: he knew it, she knew it, and his father would have known it if he hadn't been sleeping with her. "Out the way. Let me look."

While some of his staff ran around the hotel trying to find a technician, and yet others hovered close by, silently nervous, Malek sat at the computer and tried to fathom where the document had gone. But it was nowhere to be found. He grunted with frustration. It seemed his EA was good at something—and that was making the most important document of his life disappear without trace.

He rose and paced to the window. The last thing he wanted was his country, already the weakest link in the Desert Kings alliance since the death of his father, to be seen as an unprofessional, inefficient laughing stock.

He turned once more to his EA who had resumed tapping the keys as if it would conjure up something. "If you can't fix this problem, get someone who can. Immediately!" He glanced around. "And get someone to clear up these cups. Do I have to oversee everything around here?"

He flung open the windows. The roar of Paris traffic filled the air but did nothing to stem his rising impatience. Was he surrounded by idiots?

Another look made him he realize he was. The number of people had doubled as they scratched their heads, and talked volubly and irritably on their phones.

"Where's the computer technician for the hotel?"

They shrugged. He turned to the young woman who was tidying up the coffee cups. "You! Where's the computer technician?"

The woman glanced behind her before clearing her throat. "He's not here, sir. I mean... Your Royal Highness... sir." She blushed with confusion.

He narrowed his gaze and she looked away and continued to tidy the cups. Odd. Someone as beautiful as this young woman, who could have been a model, was a servant.

"Your Royal Highness!" one of his men called.

Forgetting the woman, he turned to his man and walked over. "Have you fixed it?"

"Yes, I think so."

All eyes were on the screen when a document appeared. There was a general sigh of relief from everyone... except Malek.

"That's not it. That's an earlier version. There's no time to re-write it. If it's deleted, it'll still be on the hard drive. Find it!"

There was a pause followed by an uncomfortable clearing of a throat as the bravest of his assistants prepared to break the news. "I don't think we can, Your Royal Highness. It's impossible."

"It's not impossible," said a voice from behind. "I can find it for you."

The voice, with its strong English accent, was so soft he wouldn't have noticed it if it weren't for the look of derision from his staff as they looked over to the servant clearing the table. He followed their combined, disbelieving gaze.

"If you like, I can have a look," she said tentatively.

One of his men waved a dismissive hand at her. But there was something in her quiet composure which made Malek pause.

He nodded to her. "See what you can do."

Her cheeks were suffused with color, making her brown eyes appear redder, almost tawny, he noted as she walked over to the computer.

She sat on the vacated chair and peered at the screen for a few moments.

"What's the document called?"

She swiftly entered a series of commands as she received the answer from one of his assistants. She flicked between screens quickly. "And... was it updated last night?" She addressed her question to him, rather than one of his assistants, as if she understood what dolts they were.

"That's right. Last night," he confirmed.

She double-clicked on an icon, and stood, as his missing document appeared on the screen. There was a collective gasp and grumbling as his staff came to terms with the fact that a servant had done something they couldn't do.

He barked orders at his men who scattered, returning to their positions, as the doors opened and the other kings and their entourages entered.

Malek looked at the woman who was working quickly to finish wiping the table and clear the used cups, her long, dark ponytail swinging as she moved.

His eyes lingered before he made sure the rest of the afternoon's presentations were in order. By the time he looked up again, she'd gone.

He turned to Maryam, who was now reseated in the AV booth. "I want her on my staff immediately."

Her beautiful brow furrowed. "But we don't need another cleaner."

"As my new executive assistant. Consider yourself dismissed."

SOPHIE HADN'T EVEN HAD time to put the dirty cups into the dishwasher when Monsieur Claude appeared, looking more harassed than before, if that were possible.

"Sophie!"

"I'm sorry. But they wanted the room cleared, and there wasn't anyone else here so—"

"Sophie. Be quiet. Leave that. And get back into the boardroom. You're wanted in there."

"But... But... Why?"

"You tell me," he said grimly, eyeing her up and down. "Apparently you impressed the crown prince, and he now wants you... in some capacity or other."

Sophie sat as if a hand had pushed her down.

"But... I don't understand."

"And nor do I. We're not paid to understand. We just do as we're told. I don't know why you're wanted, I didn't ask. Whatever the Crown Prince of Sumaira wants, he gets."

There was something in the snide, suggestive way Monsieur Claude said this that made her look up, suddenly indignant. "I helped him with a computer problem he had. That's all."

"Well, whatever it was, he was impressed and his staff told me that he wants you in the boardroom immediately." He held out a state-of-the-art cell phone. "Apparently it's all in here."

"What's all in here?"

"How the hell should I know?" He thrust the cell phone into her hands. "Take that apron off and go. *Now*! One of his officials is waiting for you in the royal suite."

Sophie untied the apron, and Monsieur Claude snatched it from her and pushed her out the door. She walked quickly toward the royal suite but once outside the double doors emblazoned with the gold crown motif, she hesitated. She took a deep breath, smoothed her dress and knocked.

"Enter!"

An official wearing traditional robes and a deep frown opened the door. "Sit there"—he indicated a seat in front of a computer—"and complete these checks and tests."

"Checks?"

"Security."

She began reading through the screen. "Just for one afternoon's work?"

The official ignored her question. "Once you've completed the formalities, check the cell phone. Your duties are spelled out there. I'll be back shortly and I'll take you to the meeting room. His Royal Highness wishes you to prepare a presentation from some of his notes." He glanced at his watch. "I'll return in ten minutes."

Before she could ask any other questions, he'd disappeared. She shrugged and began completing the forms. What was it to her? She had nothing to hide and this was better than washing dirty crockery and scrubbing grimy surfaces.

FOR THE REST of the afternoon she worked alone in a small room off the main meeting room. Every now and then someone would enter and hand her a memory stick, and she'd hear the drone of voices as the meeting continued. Then the door would click closed and she was alone once more to work on what had been given her, and to check the phone for further instructions on what to do with it.

It was late in the evening by the time she stood and rolled her shoulders, automatically doing the exercises that she'd learned were vital when she'd worked from home on computers. She walked over to the window and pushed it open, needing to feel the fresh night air on her face.

The door clicked open again. "Just leave it on the desk," she said with a sigh. She propped her elbows on the windowsill and stretched her back, rested her chin on her hands and breathed deeply, waiting for the nameless man to depart, as usual without speaking to her.

But the click didn't come. "Leave what? Do you think I've brought refreshments?"

She jumped up, stumbling away from the window, nearly tripping as she realized it was the voice of the crown prince himself.

"I'm sorry, sir—"

"Your Royal Highness."

"But…" she said, suddenly confused.

"*That* is what you may address me as." He strode into the room and up to the window. "And what is it that is so absorbing out the window?"

"Nothing sir… Your Royal Highness. Just fresh air."

He stood at the open window, and she could have sworn that some of the tension in his face relaxed a little. Then he looked at her. "My prime vizier tells me that, as well as working on the tasks I've given you, you've offered suggestions for the redesign of the workflow systems."

"They were a bit clunky before."

"*Clunky.*"

"In any case, I tweaked them a little. They'll work better now."

"You… *tweaked* them? And how were you able to get past our security systems?"

"It wasn't hard. I'm sorry, I didn't mean any harm." She shrugged. "It's just that I can't bear seeing inelegant programming."

"Do you know how much my father paid for this 'clunky' design?"

"No, but I can guess."

He didn't say anything for a moment, just looked at her in that inscrutable way of his. "I don't need you to guess. What I *need* is your help. If you have plans for the next few months, Miss…"

"Brown." She suddenly realized that he didn't even know her name.

"Miss Brown, cancel them. The coming months are critical for my country. I can have nothing go wrong. *Nothing.* I need the best. And when it comes to IT, apparently you're it. You are to work for me."

Crown prince or not, his peremptory command irked her. "I am?"

"Yes. My staff will work out the details of your contract."

"I have a job here. I'll have to give notice."

"No, you won't."

"Won't I?"

"No. My family owns the hotel."

She suddenly realized how out of her depth she was. This man was more powerful than she'd imagined. The thought sent a shiver along her spine. "My duties… what will they be?"

"Whatever I require."

She took a deep, shuddering breath, trying to ignore her quickening heartbeat, the fizzing of attraction low in her gut, and, most disconcertingly, an instinctive lowering of her gaze to his lips. They weren't full lips, but sensuous, even so. Then they quirked slightly. She raised her eyes to his, suddenly aware of what she was doing.

"I take it you don't have a problem with that?" he continued.

He knew. He'd seen her instinctive reaction to him. No doubt he could run roughshod over everyone, using his looks and power. "Actually, I do. The job description is a little too broad for me."

"Is it indeed? And why is that?" Gone was any sign of

amusement. His voice was as hard, cold, and unyielding as steel. As were his eyes.

She shook her head, desperately trying to think clearly and speak diplomatically. "Because we're living in the twenty-first century where people have job descriptions... and the like."

"And the like," he repeated, his chill tone sending shivers through her. "Do you fear that I will make you do something unpleasant?" He stepped closer and Sophie immediately wished he hadn't. She was of average height but he was tall... She looked up as he approached... Very tall. And the way he looked her up and down... it did something very strange to her stomach, and lower.

She shrugged as nonchalantly as a rapidly beating heart and surging adrenaline would allow. "Probably not. But I think it's only right that I know, only right that I'm told all my duties in advance."

He was so close now that she could see a muscle twitch in his jaw as if there was some inner tension, as if he weren't as cold as he appeared. His gaze briefly ranged over her face. "And what, I wonder, is it that makes you so different from others on my staff?"

She swallowed under his scrutiny. "I doubt I am. Surely they want to know what they're agreeing to."

He shook his head, once. "No. Not if money is involved. It seems, Miss..."

"Brown," she said once more.

"That you are different. And I certainly don't object to that." His vivid blue eyes glittered in the light from a multitude of table lamps. "For the next six months, you will work on my personal IT systems and other projects as required. You will not discuss your work with anyone. You will report directly to me. What I want, Miss Brown, is for you to ensure my life runs smoothly. To do whatever is required to make this happen."

"*Whatever* is required?" she repeated.

"I think you misunderstand me. I want you for your computer skills, your organizational efficiency, and your research skills."

"To?"

"Be one step ahead so I'm never in a situation like I was today. Are these terms suitable for you?"

She didn't miss the sarcasm in his tone but nodded, her heart still racing at his proximity, and at the intensity in his gaze.

"Excellent. And you will also be available at a moment's notice. You will reside in the palace. And you won't take any leave of absence during this time. Except if you're sick of course."

"No holidays?"

"You can take as much leave as you like after your work has concluded. I'll have the papers prepared for your signature."

"No."

"No?" He frowned, as if unused to that response.

She cleared her throat. "No. I'm traveling. I'm not staying in place more than a few months."

He sighed. "Six months working for me and you'll have earned enough money to go to wherever you wish, to do whatever you like."

She chewed her lip as her mind raced. She'd had to source her work through an agency so she could work from home, and the agency had cheated her. She needed money. And she didn't exactly have many options. He was right. "Okay. I agree."

"Good. I want you to complete what you're working on

and come to the bar at ten o'clock this evening to meet my prime vizier. He has a few things to go over with you."

"Yes, of course."

He opened the door, paused, and turned to her. "And... thank you."

She looked up and couldn't prevent a smile. He didn't look the type of man to recognize service, more the type to expect it.

"You look surprised, Miss Brown."

"Well, a bit."

"I'm pleased with your work. I'm pleased with the way you saved my face. I'm pleased with the fact I'll not have to concern myself with 'clunky' systems anymore."

"Oh... I'm, I'm pleased... that you're pleased..." she stammered.

His eyes narrowed. "You're blushing, Miss Brown. Do you receive compliments so rarely?"

She shrugged awkwardly. "From royalty, anyway."

For a brief moment she thought she saw his lips twist slightly before he went out the room. She was left looking at the closed door, wondering if what she'd seen was a smile... wondering if she'd done the right thing... wondering if she'd just traded her freedom for imprisonment.

CHAPTER 2

*S*ophie checked her watch again. Ten on the dot. She stepped out the elevator with a confidence she didn't feel. Give her a computer and she was in her element, but mixing with strangers—and royal strangers at that—had her stomach tied in knots and her mouth dry with fear.

You can do it, she muttered under her breath. But with each click of her high heels on the marble floor, Sophie felt her confidence wane. By the time she'd reached the entrance to the bar, she was on the verge of turning back. What in this world had induced her to wear such a fitting red dress? Yes, with its over-the-knee length and high neck it was discreet enough, but what she hadn't taken into account was the fact she'd filled out a little over the past month, and it now left very little to the imagination.

Nervously, she tried to pluck the fine material away from her curves as she peered inside the bar. It was full. She inhaled deeply and stood tall. She knew what had induced her to wear the dress. The same instinct which had seen her applying bright red lipstick. She needed to show everyone, not least herself, that she hadn't compromised her freedom in accepting this job.

The bar was discreetly lit, for which Sophie was thankful as she slipped into the room behind a large contingent of the Crown Prince of Sumaira's guests. She grabbed a couple of canapés and a glass of wine from the table and slipped unnoticed into a dark corner. From there she could see everyone and wait for this minister guy to appear.

"Mademoiselle Sophie?"

She looked up to find the bar manager, Antoine, had appeared carrying a tray of wine, water, and several plates with lids on them.

"Wow! This smells delicious." She sniffed appreciatively, suddenly aware of how hungry she was. "Thank you! That's so kind of you."

He lifted an eyebrow. "It wasn't me, Sophie, I was asked to bring you some refreshments." He set down the contents of the tray and removed the lids from the plates.

"Um," she sighed appreciatively, suddenly aware of how hungry she was. "Was it the prime vizier who sent it?" She glanced across the bar. The crown prince was talking to a group of people, completely unaware of her. "Which one is he? I'm meant to meet him."

"Not the prime vizier, Sophie. Only the crown prince himself." He grinned and winked.

She took a mouthful and chewed thoughtfully as she looked across to the crown prince. Could he have? No, Antoine must have it wrong. She shrugged. "Whoever it was, this is really good."

She watched Antoine return to the bar and let her gaze stray back to the crown prince. Had he really ordered this food for her? It was hardly likely. She'd understood from the work she'd been doing all afternoon and late into the evening that this meeting was incredibly important to him and his

country. That since his brother's disappearance and his
father's sudden death, only weeks earlier, he'd had to step
into a role which, as younger brother, he hadn't been
groomed for. He would hardly have had time to think of
anything else. No, Antoine must have it wrong.

She continued to eat and watch, taking the opportunity to
assess the people she'd be working with, the world she was
about to enter. A world as foreign to her as anything
could be.

It seemed she wasn't the only person who had been
working late. A hush fell on the room as a group of six men
entered the bar, all wearing Western dress—sharply cut suits
—all impressive in different ways. She recognized them from
the brief glimpses she'd had in the meeting room and some
research she'd done on the internet.

First was King Zahir, grim looking and serious. Sophie
knew that having been king and a fighter for much of his life,
he was well-respected for his political and defense expertise.
Even if he weren't, thought Sophie, just looking at him would
be enough to make you respect him. He was walking beside
his younger brother who hadn't been at the meeting. Slighter
than the king and less impressive, he looked a little lost,
Sophie thought. But then beside King Zahir anyone would
look lost.

Directly behind them were the royalty from Sitra—the
king and both sons. The youngest son, Razeen, thought
Sophie, looked most at home in the Parisian hotel. He looked
around the bar with a smile full of charm that only the man
he was chatting to could compete with. That man was
Sahmir, the youngest brother in the kingdom of Ma'in. His
two brothers, King Tariq and crown prince Daidan
completed the powerhouse group informally known as the
"Desert Kings."

Malek rose to greet them. Between Sophie and the group

were the bodyguards and officials. None of them women, she noted. So much testosterone in a room could make a girl giddy.

She focused on finishing her dinner, which, she had to admit, was the best she'd eaten in a long time when suddenly she was aware of someone standing over her.

"*Bonsoir, mademoiselle!*" She looked up into a face that was even more handsome close to. Prince Sahmir of Ma'in stood before her.

"*Bonsoir,*" she replied automatically, mentally trying to think what honorific she should have added.

"You are English?" he said reverting to English.

"Is my accent so bad?" She couldn't help but smile. Sahmir was by far the most approachable of any of these royals.

"No, not bad. Charmingly English," he said. "May I join you?"

The idea of saying "no" didn't cross Sophie's mind. "Sure."

He sat and poured her a glass of champagne from the bottle he was holding and one for himself. Then he lifted his glass to hers. "Let's drink."

She raised her glass. There was something so light-hearted and charming and irresistible about him that she couldn't help but respond. "What are we drinking to?"

"Why, to the most beautiful woman in the room."

Sophie glanced around and laughed. "Perhaps we could also drink to 'the only woman in the room?'"

"Why not? Both are correct. But I'm sure that even if the room were full of women, the first toast would remain accurate."

The heated blush rose through her body as the glasses clinked and she took a sip of her champagne. Sahmir was handsome and very engaging, no doubt about that, but being unused to such attention she wished she'd had the courage to refuse his offer of company. She looked around, hoping for rescue from this inveterate charmer with whom she was hopelessly out of her depths. She caught the intense gaze of Crown Prince Malek briefly before Sahmir attracted her attention once more.

"And what is an English rose doing in Paris? On holiday?"

"Working."

"Really? Are you a model?"

The blush deepened if anything and Sophie shook her head. "No, *not*. Definitely not a model."

"Then what is it you do?"

"She works for me," a deep, firm voice answered.

They both looked up to see Malek standing over them.

Sahmir didn't miss a beat. He rose. "Ah, I should have guessed." Malek didn't look at Sophie, but cast a challenging eye at Sahmir.

"Really?"

Sophie looked from one to the other of them. She sensed some underlying tension between them. Malek's devastatingly handsome face showed no good humor, unlike Sahmir's.

"Of course." Sahmir's lips curled into a smile that Sophie felt hid something more. "And tell me, how is Judge Vignon?"

Malek's gaze was cool and inscrutable. "I couldn't tell you."

Sophie noticed a slight narrowing of Sahmir's eyes, as if he were baiting Malek. "Really? A delightful lady, known to her friends as Veronique. And you are her friend, I believe?"

"As a public figure, Judge Vignon has many friends," Malek replied evasively.

Sahmir raised one eyebrow and huffed, as if suddenly understanding something. He rose, picked up his glass and looked quizzically at Malek. "I didn't realize..." Sahmir looked at Sophie and his grin broadened. "It was lovely meeting you, Sophie, no matter how briefly."

"And you," she muttered, regretting she'd been swayed by her need to appear super-confident and worn her red dress. She felt more vulnerable than confident now.

Malek watched Sahmir leave and turned to Sophie, looking directly into her eyes, unlike Sahmir whose eyes had lingered over her figure. "Are you okay?"

"Yes, thank you. The dinner was lovely." She winced inwardly. It sounded a feeble thing to say to an Adonis who was enquiring after her welfare.

"Good." He stepped away. "I thought you might be hungry after working so late."

She must have shown her surprise, because there was that subtle quirk of his lips, which she now realized was as close to a smile as he got. "I'll leave you to your dessert." He nodded at the elaborate dessert she'd been tempted by. "My staff has informed you of your travel plans tomorrow?"

"Yes. Thank you."

"Good." He walked away before turning. "And Miss Brown?"

"Yes?"

"Thank you for stepping in at such short notice. It's appreciated." He stepped away, his gaze still holding hers. "My vizier will be free to see you shortly."

She looked at her drink to hide her blushes. She felt as if he'd caressed her, not thanked her for her work. Get a grip, she told herself sternly.

It wasn't until some time after she'd finished her dessert that the prime vizier beckoned her over. He rose—exotic and out of place in the Paris hotel—to greet her in an old-fashioned show of respect. Despite the forbidding sweep of robes and heavy beard, his eyes were kindly in a face worn by the elements.

"Please, be seated." She sat in the chair opposite as he'd indicated. He observed her silently and she looked around, uncomfortable. The crown prince was talking with the other kings, and no one was paying them any attention. "You've done well this afternoon for the crown prince, and for the other Desert Kings. We are all appreciative of your work."

"You're welcome."

"And you are ready to leave with us tomorrow?"

"Yes. I travel light."

"Good. Report to the lobby first with your luggage and then His Royal Highness, the crown prince, will require your assistance."

"Of course." She paused, waiting to hear why he wanted to see her. But he didn't say anything, simply continued to look at her in an assessing way. "Was there anything else, sir?"

"No. I simply wished to see you in these surroundings."

She frowned. "Oh?"

But he ignored her implied question and waved her away with a kindly smile. "You may go."

She rose, confused. She had no idea why he'd wanted to see her, or what had just happened, if anything. "Thank you."

But instead of leaving by the main door, on impulse she went to the bar and slipped out the rear to join Antoine and the other waiters and kitchen hands she'd come to know. Someone opened a bottle of wine and glasses were poured.

"To Sophie. Swept off her feet by a king."

She grinned and accepted the glass. "Not a king. Not yet anyway."

One glass turned into another and it was past midnight before she looked at her watch again. "I have to go and pack. We're leaving tomorrow. Night, everyone."

Without thinking, she went out the way she came, into the bar which now seemed deserted. She stopped suddenly, aware of two men talking still, at the bar. It was Malek, sitting thoughtfully, listening to his prime vizier. Malek looked up when Sophie entered the room. He exchanged brief words with the other man and then rose and came over to her.

"Would you care for a night-cap?"

She was about to say no, but something in his eyes, something more real than she'd seen in them all day, made her nod. "Yes, that would be nice."

He ordered the drink and gave her a quick, sweeping glance. He exchanged looks with his vizier who was watching them thoughtfully, before turning to her. "I think we will work well together, Miss Brown."

"Sophie, please."

"Sophie."

A shiver tracked through her as she watched his sensual lips say her name, like a whisper of desire.

"Sophie." He said it again. This time, it did something more. She took a deep breath, trying to control her treacherous body. "The wise one," he added. "And I've a feeling you are." For the first time the hard, cold barrier dropped from his eyes. Although his lips didn't move from their set position, a warmth filled his blue eyes that was all the more powerful for its brevity and suddenness, for the contrast to their usual cool. And she realized how much he hid from the world.

He ignored a brief cough from his vizier as the night bartender emerged with her drink. He tapped his glass against hers with a clink. "Your health." But before he could take a sip, a phone rang and his vizier called him over. He glanced around and when he looked back at her that breach in his guard had gone. He was royalty once more.

"I must go. Until tomorrow."

She retreated to a shadowy corner with the drink she suddenly realized she didn't want. At that moment King Zahir strode into the room. His tall, broad frame seemed to dominate the empty bar. Sophie sensed a sadness in his step that she'd not noticed before.

Still on the phone, Malek acknowledged Zahir who moved over to the bar, ordered a drink, and stood, lost in thought.

Then a tall, classy, beautiful blonde stepped hesitantly into the bar, wearing a fitting black dress over her long, slender body, subtle low-heeled pumps, and jewelry. The bar was private and so the woman must have been a member of the Desert Kings contingent but Sophie hadn't seen her before. She must have arrived later than the others.

The woman looked around as if searching for someone; her face fell. King Zahir saw her and she looked as if she'd been electrified. Zahir had the same expression on his face. He straightened and she walked toward him, as if impelled by some external force.

Sophie couldn't take her eyes off them. They stood apart not speaking. Sophie frowned. What was going on? Then he offered her a drink and a seat at the bar which she accepted. They hardly spoke, but their eyes and their gestures gave them away. Little by little they moved toward each other. Sophie thought that if had been possible to make love without making love, she'd never seen anything closer to it. The two of them were practically devouring each other with their eyes. Then he took her hand and drove his fingers into hers. They gripped their joined fists and without saying anything further they left their drinks on the bar and walked out together, oblivious to anyone around them. Sophie's eyes followed them to the elevator. They stepped in and before the doors slid closed, they'd come together in a kiss that sizzled with passion.

Arousal filled Sophie in that split second in which she'd seen them come together. Her skin tingled, her breathing came shorter, and she felt a throbbing between her legs. She swallowed and shifted a little before looking away, straight into the eyes of Malek. Blue eyes. Intense eyes. Aroused eyes, same as hers must be.

Her face burned with sexual desire and embarrassment. She grabbed her bag and stood. Without looking at him she walked, acutely aware of the sexual sway of her hips in the high shoes, to the lobby, and the staff elevator which would take her to her room, feeling his eyes boring into her all the time.

What was he thinking? Of how badly she compared to the beautiful blonde with whom King Zahir was obviously about to spend a passionate night? No doubt. But still... that look in his eyes. She couldn't, she *mustn't*, think about that.

She stepped into the empty elevator and swiped the card which would take her to the staff quarters. No. All she could think about was that she'd gotten exactly what she'd planned and hoped for—travel with no emotional attachments. No one and nothing to tie her down, beyond a few months. And at the end of those months she'd be free to move on and would have the money to do so. But what she couldn't have anticipated was the heat that throbbed in her, the flutter of sensation that skittered down her spine and straight to parts she'd spent years *not* thinking about, whenever Malek looked at her. That, most definitely, was not part of her plan.

CHAPTER 3

A vision of chaos greeted Sophie as she stepped out of the elevator the next day, clutching the smart laptop bag which contrasted so vividly with her ancient, battered suitcase. There were people everywhere, calling out orders, with fewer people available to carry them out.

She glanced anxiously at her watch. She'd been instructed to report to the foyer. She walked up to one of the men she recognized from the day before.

"*Excusez-moi.* Where should I go? Where should I put my bag?"

She was rewarded with a look of annoyance. "Not here! This is for the coach passengers." He waved his hand dismissively.

"Then where?"

"You'll be traveling with the crown prince. You are his new assistant, are you not?"

She nodded.

"Then, of course, you'll be traveling with him. Go. His office will take care of your things."

"The crown prince?" She paused as she tried to control

the strange flutterings in her stomach that had stirred at his name. "I'm traveling with the crown prince?"

The man scowled. "You would question his command?"

She frowned and shook her head in response. "No, of course not. Thank you." She walked toward the suite of rooms where she knew she'd find the man whose very name made her heart pound with anticipation.

She knocked at the door of the suite and waited. There was no reply. She knocked again, and a harried looking man swung open the door. He muttered something unintelligible when he saw her and ushered her impatiently in, pushing the door closed behind her.

"Hurry! His Royal Highness has been asking for you."

"But I wasn't told…"

"Do you have to be told everything? You are in the employ of the Crown Prince of Sumaira now. Your time is not your own."

She frowned. What the hell was she getting herself into? But before she could respond, a side door opened and a beautiful woman in her late thirties emerged. She didn't see Sophie. The woman closed the door behind her, stopped, and took a deep breath. She looked at the floor and Sophie saw a tear roll down her averted cheek. It was quickly swiped away as she stood tall, and pulled out a cell phone and began giving instructions in French to someone who was obviously her junior. Still talking, she walked away, down the private staircase, the epitome of poise and sophistication.

Who was she? Whoever it was, she'd been able to contain her emotions as easily as flicking a switch.

Just at that moment the harried looking assistant came round the corner. "There you are! Not that entrance, that's His Royal Highness's private entrance. This way!" He waved his hand and Sophie followed him through an anteroom and suddenly found herself standing before the crown prince who looked up at her from beneath a lowered brow.

"You're late."

"Mal—" she stopped herself just in time from saying the name she'd been thinking of him by. "I mean sir—"

"It's Your Royal Highness," he said smoothly, with a resigned air.

"I'm sorry, sir—Your Royal—"

He waved his hand. "It doesn't matter. I've been held up."

Sophie couldn't help thinking that "being held up" hadn't brought a tear to *his* eye. "What would you like me to do?"

"Sit and begin work." He glanced at his watch. "We have half an hour before we leave and a lot to do."

She opened the laptop she'd been given the day before, and began noting the instructions Malek issued. She could hear tension in his voice, but not in his choice of words. Maybe she'd been wrong? Maybe he *had* been affected by the woman and was simply as controlled as she'd been.

"Any more emails?"

Sophie scanned the last one and hesitated.

"Yes?"

"One has come in from the prime vizier. He reminds you that you have to…" She couldn't quite bring herself to relay the vizier's suggestion.

"To what?"

She looked up into his serious, grim face. "To smile when we land in Sumaira."

He grunted, held her gaze for a moment.

"My prime vizier thinks I lack charm."

"Oh," she exhaled, thinking only another man could think a man this gorgeous needed charm.

"Apparently I don't smile enough. And it seems I need to smile to win over my people." He paused, searching her face. "Would you agree with his assessment?"

She shook her head before she had time to form a considered response.

"No? Interesting. You do not think my features too hard to evoke warm feelings from my countrymen... and women?"

Again, she shook her head.

"You may speak frankly, Sophie. I would value your opinion, particularly if it is opposite to my vizier's. I am not keen to transform myself into a grinning fool. So... do you believe my expression needs amending?"

She could sense in his tone that he truly wanted to know.

"No." She glanced at the lines of his jaw and cheekbones. They were without softness—strong and uncompromising, but not hard. She cleared her throat. "Surely..." She hesitated as she thought how best to express herself. "Surely a king needs to be strong, and you have a strong face. Not hard." How could his minister not see the passion and energy that he restrained? It was there in his eyes, his lips...

They gazed at each other for long seconds and then he rose and walked around the desk. She busied herself with the laptop. But she could feel his presence as he approached her.

"So maybe I can safely ignore my vizier's advice, for once."

She nodded, gazing fixedly in front of her at the laptop.

She felt his hand on her arm, and she closed her eyes and sucked in a sharp breath.

"Thank you for your honesty. I..."

Whatever else he was about to say was stopped by the door being flung open suddenly as a woman of around sixty swept into the room followed by a flurry of security guards who were trying to stop her. The woman's imperious gaze halted their efforts more effectively than a physical blow.

"I'm sorry, Your Royal Highness..." spluttered the assistant.

Sophie looked from the impeccably groomed woman back to Malek whose face had suddenly changed into an expression which Sophie could now call nothing but hard.

"Leave us," barked Malek at the guards. The guards quickly left and Sophie also rose to go. "Stay," Malek growled without glancing her way. "The lady won't be here long."

Sophie looked at the woman, whose face was ablaze with anger.

"What the hell's going on?" the woman said in a low, insistent voice. Her designer suit fitted her slender figure like a glove. She moved with the conscious grace of a woman used to being admired. She stopped in front of the desk and folded her arms, her manicured nails drumming on the midnight blue silk of her arm. "You tricked me." Her voice was all the more menacing for its quietness.

Malek rose and walked around the desk and stood over her, apparently not in the least intimidated by this magnificent woman.

"I did nothing of the sort."

"The summit was scheduled for *next* week."

Malek shrugged. "It was changed."

"You didn't tell me. You didn't advise me of the changes."

"There was no need."

"You knew I wanted to attend."

"It wasn't necessary."

"It was to me. You did this on purpose, didn't you?"

"I do everything on purpose. The summit was too important for anyone to think our country's leadership is divided."

"Better to be divided than weak!" She snorted. "You're like your father. Look what a mess his reign got us into."

Sophie took advantage of the sharp cut and thrust of the dialogue to quietly rise from the desk and skirt the arguing couple. But the woman turned to her, and Sophie recoiled under her sharp gaze.

"And who's this? You *are* like him, aren't you? Picking up mistresses while your bed is still warm from your old one. I'd have thought you'd taken Prime Vizier Mohammed's suggestions about marrying to heart. He is a wise man, your father's best friend, and he'll be yours, too. I suggest you do as he tells you, and marry."

"And I suggest you leave."

"I'm leaving. I'm returning to Sumaira. And I'll see you there. This isn't the end. I may have missed out on the summit but I don't intend to watch someone as inexperienced as you take control of my country."

"*Our* country," Malek corrected. "And I'm not going to let you within an inch of any real power. Those days are gone."

"The country needs its king to be strong and all this diplomacy, all this running around talking, isn't going to get us anywhere, isn't going to make the threat from the east go away."

"I want you to leave. *Now.* I can't risk the Desert Kings Accord being undermined by your influence."

The woman shook her head, her expression as steely as Malek's. "I wish your brother were here. He'd do the right thing. He'd agree with me." She glanced at Sophie. "And he wouldn't be hanging around with the likes of her. He'd be getting on with the business of marriage. *That* is what you don't understand. You'll sacrifice nothing for your country."

Sophie's heart beat rapidly as Malek approached the woman. The woman didn't flinch. She must have had nerves of steel because Malek looked positively dangerous. "I'll sacrifice everything. I *have* sacrificed everything. I suggest you leave—*now*—before I have my guards escort you off the premises."

"I'll leave. But I'll be back. Not here in Paris, but in Sumaira. This isn't the end of the matter."

The enmity between the two electrified the air. When the

woman left the room and the door shut, Malek turned to Sophie, and she saw the depth of his anger and frustration in his gaze.

He walked to his desk, gathered his papers, and closed his laptop. He paused for a moment before turning to her, his expression controlled once more. "I apologize for the intrusion."

Sophie was surprised that he'd apologize for anything. "That's okay. I didn't understand..." She trailed off.

"Understand what it was all about? I'm not surprised. It's complicated."

She opened her mouth to speak but thought better of it.

"You have a question, Sophie?"

She nodded.

He sighed and leaned against the desk. "You may ask me one, and then we must leave."

"Why did you let her talk to you like that? And why didn't she call you 'Your Royal Highness?'"

He raised an eyebrow. "Of all the questions I thought you'd ask, that was not the one. However, in answer to your most pressing question, no, she's within her rights not to call me 'Your Royal Highness'?"

"Why? Surely all your subjects should?"

"*You* don't."

"No, but..." Again she tried to stop herself from speaking her mind. But he inclined his head, as if encouraging her to continue. "But I'm not your subject. Well, only for the next six months."

"And you think that gives you dispensation to not call me by my title?"

"I'm sorry, Your Royal—"

"I think we're a little beyond that now. *Sir* is fine as it's all you can seem to remember. Now, if you still care to work for me, I suggest we leave. We've a plane to catch."

She winced at her faux pas. She hated any questioning of her memory after living with her mother's dementia. She knew her mother's form of the disease wasn't hereditary, but still the fear lingered.

But he didn't move. "Do you?"

"Sorry?"

"Still wish to work for me?"

Part of her wanted to say no. To say that the scene she'd just witnessed had scared the heck out of her was the understatement of the year. In her small world, there had been few arguments and any disagreements between friends or family soon blew over. Least said, soonest mended, had been her mother's motto. And Sophie's too. But there was a look in Malek's eye that called to her. His eyes still held a flare of anger, betraying how hard it was for him to contain the passion that lurked beneath that impassive exterior.

"Yes."

His frown lessened slightly. "Then we must leave now."

She grabbed her bag as the door was opened by his assistant.

Malek looked up at him. "Is everything prepared?"

"Yes, Your Royal Highness."

"Then go." The door closed behind his assistant and they were alone. "I'm pleased you've accepted the job. As you can see, there is much work to be done. And I need reliable staff. People I can trust." She walked over to the open door. "And I can trust you, can't I?"

"Yes." She paused, still desperately wanting to know more about the strange scene, but reluctant to ask. But she had to ask. She needed to know as much as she could about what she was letting herself in for. "But how come that woman was allowed to come into your office? Surely your guards could have stopped her?"

He glanced around the tidy room and indicated that she

should precede him which surprised her. But this was a man who had never been groomed to be king and, she guessed, old habits died hard.

"In the future, the guards *will* stop her. But I hadn't given orders for her to be stopped."

"Why not? She's obviously against you."

He closed the door firmly behind them, and they walked out into the lobby where lights flashed as stray paparazzi jostled to catch the best photo of the man who was about to be crowned King of Sumaira, together with a woman.

"Indeed, she is. But, Sophie…" They walked through the swing doors toward the waiting limo. A door opened and she stepped inside. "She isn't just any powerful, ambitious woman." The door was slammed after her as he got into the seat on the other side. "She's my mother."

As the Paris streets slid by Sophie gripped her laptop bag firmly. She looked out the window, trying to control the mixture of anger and confusion—and more than that—a deep, deep sadness. How did that work? The mother she adored was dead. And here was Malek with a mother very alive and kicking and they both patently hated each other.

As SOON AS they arrived at the airport, they were ushered straight onto the Learjet which immediately began to move. Malek went to the spacious front cabin. Sophie began to follow him but the door was closed in her face by one of the stewards. "Right," she thought to herself, as she was ushered toward the rear of the plane where the others were seated.

She hesitated as she felt all eyes upon her—distrustful, curious eyes—then followed the beckoning steward to the seat indicated. She could feel her cheeks burn as she fastened her belt, just as the taxiing plane circled at the top of the runway. Its engines roared into life and it accelerated down the runway.

The airport buildings, the boulevards, the ancient and modern mix of Paris grew smaller as they climbed steadily upward. Sophie's eyes stung as she continued to stare at the city slowly disappearing below her. Then the plane banked sharply and Paris disappeared. There was nothing but a blue emptiness below her.

She closed her eyes. She should feel scared, diving into the unknown, but somehow she didn't. The thrum of nerves inside her stomach was of excitement, not fear. She felt free for the first time in years. Free to explore, free to live a life alone, away from the sadness that had surrounded her for so long.

And she felt guilty that she should feel that way. But she knew her mother would have wanted her to do just as she was doing. Before she'd become ill, her mother had always encouraged her to take risks, to see life as an adventure. They'd talk about the things Sophie would do when she'd left university—things, like university, which had never eventuated. No, her mother wouldn't want her to feel guilt. She'd want her to live. Just *live*, fully and happily.

Sophie opened her eyes and looked around. But how to live in a place that was so different to her world, a small village in the Cotswolds? The modest cottage in which most things had been passed down from her grandparents, and their parents before them? She knew nothing of the world of luxury which surrounded her now. From the cream leather seats on which she rested her hands, to the subdued lighting which made the gold accents in the light fittings, and trim of the seats and windows, glow. Even the men, who were talking in groups around the desks, looked and sounded exotic and alien with their mahogany skin tones against the bright white of their robes, and the Arabic which they spoke.

A different world. And, for the next months at least, it was going to be her world.

As soon as the seatbelt light was extinguished, an assistant emerged from the front of the plane and came toward her.

"His Royal Highness wishes to see you, Miss Brown."

"Oh, sure." She fumbled with her belt and rose, reaching under the seat in front for the laptop bag.

The man beckoned impatiently. "Come! His Royal Highness doesn't like to be kept waiting."

The man knocked on the door and she heard a muffled response. He pushed the door open, his head lowered as he held it open for her. She stepped into the thickly carpeted office and in one glance took in the spacious luxury of the office, and the prime vizier looking at her with intense interest. He rose from his seat in front of the desk to reveal a scowling Malek behind it.

"Ah, Sophie," said the vizier, his penetrating eyes focused too intently on her. "Please, take a seat. I am leaving." He nodded at Malek, who still hadn't acknowledged Sophie. With a glance at Sophie and a smile, the vizier left the room.

Sophie went and sat in front of Malek—who kept his eyes firmly fixed on some papers in front of him—and opened the laptop she'd been using.

He glanced up, his brows knitted with irritation. "What are you doing?"

"About to start work?"

His eyes flickered to hers and shifted away. She suddenly felt uncomfortable. All the previous times they'd been together his gaze had been steady. Something had happened. Something he felt uncomfortable about.

He sighed. "It *is* work. But it doesn't require a laptop."

She frowned. "What do you mean?" If he was going to

try anything on—even if she did fancy him like crazy—there was no way in this world she was going to put up with it.

His lips twitched a little. "I mean I wish to talk. There is business to discuss. Business to transact. But nothing that requires a laptop." His lips twitched once more at her frowning response. "Don't worry. It isn't as you think. You're safe with me." Then again, the uncomfortable glance. He rose this time and strode across the room, to the cabinet upon which photo frames were ranged. He picked one up and looked at it before putting it down. He signaled it with his hand. "My father. My family."

She nodded slowly, trying to understand what he was attempting to tell her. "You wish to talk of your family?"

"In a way, yes. You need to… know things… Things which will help you to understand about me, about my country, about the role you need to play." This time he looked at her, and his gaze was steady. "Come over here."

What the hell was going on? She rose and walked over to him but stopped an arm's length away. She could smell his aftershave—masculine and enticing. She waited for him to speak. He shifted a photo from one place to another, still not looking at her. Then he sighed and looked up at her.

"We're alike, Sophie, you and I."

She was so surprised by his statement that she couldn't help a half-laugh/half-cough. "Really? In what way?"

He thrust his hands into his pockets and leaned against his desk, his gaze holding a different expression to any she'd seen before. There was no authority, no anger or irritation, only an air of resignation and, for the first time, curiosity. About her.

"You're a beautiful, smart young woman who was born into a world where your talents couldn't be appreciated."

She shook her head, frowning. "No, you're wrong." She

hesitated, unsure of how to respond to this sudden interest in her.

He raised his eyebrow. "Am I?"

"Yes, I was born into a loving family. They appreciated me."

His smile relaxed a little. "And is that enough?"

"For me, it was. And still would be. But…"

"But what? Why are you here now? I realize I know little about you, apart from what I've learned from your résumé."

She was suddenly embarrassed. How had things suddenly shifted from work to personal questions? "Why *should* you know anything?"

He shrugged. "If we are to work… *closely* with each other, it would be a good idea. Tell me about your work first of all. The agency said you worked from home for personal reasons. May I ask what these were?"

"Yes," she replied hesitantly, wondering where the conversation was headed. "So I could be with my mother. She was ill, you see. Dementia."

Malek looked genuinely surprised. "You cared for you mother? Alone?"

"Mm, yes, to begin with. Until I earned enough to pay for nursing help during the day. I could work then. I couldn't leave her, couldn't put her in an institution. You see, I'd promised her."

Surprise changed into an intense, confused frown. "You were willing to sacrifice yourself for your mother?"

"There was no sacrifice," she said indignantly. "Now, was there a reason you wanted to know this?"

Malek picked up a piece of paper and glanced at it, then at another, before tossing them onto the desk. "I'm sorry to be intrusive, but I needed to know a little more about you." He continued to hold her gaze, and Sophie forgot her irritation at his questions. Her eyes burned under the contact. She wouldn't look away. She *couldn't* look away, even if she wanted to. All the power of his authority and personality was in that gaze and something more... a heat of attraction which she'd glimpsed before but which he was now making no attempt to disguise. "Sophie...I have a proposition for you."

Her heart thudded uncomfortably and she willed the heat that his gaze had stirred not to rise to her cheeks. She couldn't ignore her response to him which was primitive and strong. But she also couldn't ignore the warning signals of her brain. Had he waited until she was trapped in his plane before the real reason he wanted to employ her emerged?

"A proposition?" Her voice was strangely hoarse. She cleared her throat. "What... kind of proposition?"

As if aware of her sudden doubts and fears Malek pushed himself off the desk and walked around to the other side, and sat. "A business proposition." He indicated she should also sit.

Cautiously, she did. She crossed her arms nervously in front of her. She was alone with the all-powerful Crown Prince of Sumaira on an airplane, with every minute taking her further and further away from her home. "And if I don't agree?"

"You may take the first flight to Paris, London, wherever you wish to go. Your flight will be paid for and you'll receive more than adequate recompense for the work you've done. And... the inconvenience."

She nodded nervously. "And this proposition, I take it it's something in addition to the duties you've already outlined?"

His gaze was steady and invasive, and she had no idea what he was thinking but whatever it was, he was considering it very carefully. "Yes." He shifted in his seat and leaned his forearms onto the desk, threading his fingers and bringing his hands together on the desk. His mouth was grim. "You've gathered that my country is in the middle of a crisis. We are threatened from the east and my mother is concerned at the vacuum left by my father's sudden death and she wishes to retain as much power as she can. But that is not possible. It's dividing the country. Mohammed, my prime vizier, has suggested a plan whereby I distract attention by being seen with a woman my people will not consider to be wife material. A foreigner. No threat. A rumor that I have a love interest will enable me to do two things. Firstly, it will make people imagine I am more like my father. My father, as my mother suggested, had numerous affairs. My people had a grudging admiration for his prowess."

"Right..." Sophie said slowly, trying to think what he was getting at.

"And secondly, it will allow me to carry on with the important business of running the country and... sorting out some other details necessary for my future as king."

"Okay..." Sophie said slowly again, wondering when he was going to come to the point.

"But it will be a smokescreen, of course."

"Of course."

"So... you are all right with this?"

She sat on her chair, her brows knitted, trying to figure out what the hell he was going on about. Who the crown prince went out with was hardly her concern. Okay, she might have the tiniest crush on him—possibly more than tiny—but that wasn't any concern of his. "Sure."

"Good." Malek sat back. His relief was palpable.

"So, if you've nothing more, I'll get to work." She indicated the laptop, her brow still furrowed as she went over what he'd said, trying to make sense of it.

It was Malek's turn to look surprised. "I think we should go through some of the details of the new arrangement. Of course, there's your wardrobe to be considered."

Sophie looked at her drab suit. She'd hoped she'd get away with not spending money on more suitable clothes. It seemed she couldn't. "I'll buy some clothes when I arrive. If you could, well, give me a little advance on my pay, that is."

"That won't be necessary."

"Well, I think it might be. If you could see my bank account you'd realize—"

"Sophie! I'll have an account set up for you at whichever shops you prefer. Money won't be an issue."

"But I can't let you pay for them. It wouldn't be right. It would look…"

"As if you're a kept woman. I think that's the point."

She jumped up so suddenly that the chair fell over. "What point?"

"If you're going to *appear* to be my mistress to the whole of my country, to the world, it's only right that I cover your expenses."

"Your…mistress?"

"*Appear* is the operative word here, Sophie. You are to *appear* to be my mistress, as I've explained."

"You've explained nothing of the sort. I thought…" She closed her eyes as the true meaning of his words fell into place. She opened them slowly. "I thought you were talking about someone else. Not me."

He walked around to her. "As my vizier has suggested to me, you're perfect. You're beautiful, clever, a foreigner, no threat, no connections. And… you're here."

"So, *convenient* as well."

"Convenient. We'll be together anyway, working on the duties I'd outlined previously." He ran a hand through his hair. "And we'll simply continue to be together in the evenings and at other times when the press will be present."

"To provide the smokescreen you spoke about."

"That's correct." He held her puzzled gaze before shaking his head. "You still don't understand, do you?"

"I don't think I do."

"A relationship with someone such as yourself will remind people of the good old times when my father was king. He—shall we say—*enjoyed* the company of many women and, while some may have disapproved, most people took this as a sign of a vigorous man, a potent ruler. And this will give me time."

"To do what?"

He sighed. "For you to work on the last task that I haven't yet mentioned to you. You see... my mother was correct about one thing."

"And that was?"

He looked at her strangely. "And that's the final task you need to do for me. To work with my adviser on."

"What is it?" she said huskily. It didn't sound like her. She didn't *feel* like her. She thought, at that moment, she would do anything he asked. *Anything.*

He didn't take his eyes from hers. "While we're pretending to be lovers I want you to find me a wife."

She heard what he said, recognized the words, but didn't understand them straight away. "You..." She swallowed.

"My mother was wrong about me not sacrificing anything. I'll do anything for my country. But she was right about my need for a wife. With our relationship as a smoke-screen, I have two months to find a wife. Two months before my coronation. Two months in which to strengthen my position." He pushed a sheaf of papers across his desk. "This is the long list. Go through it and make me a short list."

She licked her lips as she tried to stem the panic at having got everything so absolutely wrong. "You want me to do this? You don't mind if someone else decides?"

"It's better if someone else decides. There's no room for emotion in this. You have a logical mind. I want you to evaluate the options and analyze them just as you have with the other projects. Systems analysis, wife analysis. Same thing."

"Right." She jumped up and scooped up the papers, keeping her head down to obscure her burning face. "Right, I'll go and make a start." She walked toward the door and reached out to open it.

"Sophie!" His voice was closer to her than she'd imagined. In her haste to get away, she hadn't heard his footsteps across the thickly piled carpet. "I can trust no one else with this. Everyone has ulterior motives. But you... Look at me, Sophie."

She shook her head. He raised his hand as if to touch her but dropped his hand by his side again. She sighed with relief and... regret. His touch would have been inappropriate; it would have wrong, and it shouldn't have been wanted... but it was.

She turned her burning cheeks to him, sure that he would understand what he'd see.

"You will do this for me? You will do everything we've talked about?"

He didn't *have* to ask her. She was in his employ. But he *had* asked her, and there was no way she could deny him. "Yes, of course."

She walked out his office, closed the door behind her and held on to it for a moment, not wanting to join all the others and their suspicious looks. No doubt the rumors had already begun to circulate. And they were rumors she had to fan the flames of, not dismiss. Her. Sophie Brown. A nobody. A nobody who was so obviously unsuitable to marry him that she was safe to have an affair with. Albeit, an imaginary one.

She took a deep breath and re-entered the main cabin and took her seat. She could feel the eyes boring into her back. She'd have to get used to it. She'd have to get used to a lot of things, she thought. Not least, that the sexiest man she'd ever met, wanted her for one personal reason only—to find him a suitable wife.

CHAPTER 4

*M*ost people, Sophie mused, grew less attractive upon acquaintance. Not more. Malek's frown deepened as he listened intently to someone on the other end of the phone, before shaking his head, rising and talking as he paced the small office on the plane.

Two of the seven hours of the flight had slid by in a series of one intense meeting after another. Malek had insisted she remain in the room throughout the meetings. He wanted her to learn what was going on. And he wanted the rumors to begin.

Every moment she spent with him was a moment in which she got to know him better—his keen intelligence, his determination to do his duty for the country he loved, and his detachment from his family. *That*, she couldn't understand.

But it wasn't only about understanding. It was about wanting. As she watched Malek thrust his fingers through his short hair, showing his frustration in his movement, but not in his controlled voice, she couldn't help but want to soothe the tense muscles in his forearm. She could imagine the feel of his skin beneath her palm. She flexed her fingers as if to make them realize they weren't actually caressing his arm, and suddenly caught his gaze.

She pressed the back of her hand to her cheek, willing it to transfer a much-needed chill to her flushed skin and looked at the laptop in front of her. She hit random keys as if she were busy doing something.

She cleared her throat and was relieved as he continued talking on the phone. Perhaps he hadn't noticed. What would he care anyway? She was nothing to him. No one except a help with the computers, a help to find his future wife, a help in providing a smokescreen for him to hide behind. She pulled open another file of suitable women and flicked through the brief dossier. She had become adept at reading behind the brief notes. Notes it was her job to add detail to.

She sighed as she read through the file and glanced at the covering list of requirements, thanking heaven that Malek had crossed out the requirements that his wife be a virgin. How she would have confirmed *that*, she had no idea. But the other things on the list were easier to assess. Malek had made it clear he wanted someone capable and intelligent, as well as the requisite beautiful and good connections. Judging by this particular woman's history, Malek would annihilate her in conversation within minutes.

She flipped to another page. Hm, this was more like it. The woman's face was aloof, superior, and beautiful. And, as Sophie scanned the notes about her, she could see that she probably had a right to be superior. Her academic qualifications only outshone her family and tribal contacts. She looked at the woman's face once more. She was everything that Sophie wasn't. She'd be perfect for the role of Queen of Sumaira.

"How is your work going?"

Sophie jumped. She hadn't noticed Malek approach. She

glanced at the photo of the woman and quickly closed the laptop. This woman might be perfect on paper but somehow she wanted to keep her under wraps for the moment. More research to do, she justified to herself. A lot more.

Sophie looked up. "Fine."

He narrowed his eyes as he looked at her and tossed the phone onto his desk. "I hope it's better than mine." He glanced angrily at the phone.

"Anything I can help you with?"

He huffed. "I wish it were as easy as pressing a few computer buttons."

"Easy? If it were so easy then you wouldn't have had to hire me." She grimaced. It seemed so natural to be with him she kept forgetting herself. "Sorry, I shouldn't have said that…"

He grunted with amusement and waved his hand in a dismissive gesture. She looked away, out the small cabin window, but there was nothing to see. It was still night. No clouds, no orange sky to break up the star-sprinkled vast expanse of inky black.

He followed her gaze. "We have several hours more of flying. You should rest."

"I'm fine."

A slight smile still played on his lips. "Are you? Or are you wondering *where* you should rest? Wondering what's in store for you at the other end?"

She pressed her lips together in a brief, embarrassed grimace. "All of the above."

"What's awaiting you the other end is unimaginable to you, I should think. You will be bombarded with attention. It will be easier to deal with if you're rested."

"Right."

"And the only place to rest will be my bedroom. All the other space is full of my staff, whose curiosity is probably no less than the media awaiting you." He held up his hand and smiled, obviously reacting to her look. "I promise your virtue will be safe with me. Go, now." He indicated the door at the rear of the plane.

Sophie ached to the bone with tiredness. The late night, the stress of the last days had taken their toll. What Malek was saying made sense. "Are you sure you don't want to use it?"

"No. Rest now, because there will be a lot to do when we arrive."

"Sure." She flashed a brief uncertain smile and headed for the door. He was watching her, she knew. She didn't turn around. Not when she opened the door and not when she was closing it. But she knew. She could feel it as surely as if he had swept his hands over the length of her body. She closed the door and lay on the bed—his bed—and wondered what the hell she'd let herself in for.

"Sophie." Her name came to her through the mists of sleep, like the whisper of someone long forgotten. She rolled her head to one side of the snowy white pillow. "Sophie." The name came again. Then a touch. Eyes still closed, still immersed in the memory of dreams, she smiled at the brief caress, so gentle. She moaned lightly and wriggled with pleasure.

Then the hand moved, the fingers stroking her forearm briefly before retracting. It was the absence of the touch which finally made her aware of the low roar of the plane, the subdued voices outside, and the fine linen beneath her cheek. She opened her eyes and saw out the cabin window the first strands of red in the sky, and suddenly realized where she was. She twisted around in fright. Malek stood there, hands in pockets, watching her.

"I apologize, but it was necessary to wake you." She started to get out of bed but he stopped her with the touch of his hand. "Please, continue to rest. But my adviser has wisely suggested we get to know each other a little better if we are to convince others that we… That we have a relationship. And we don't have much time. We'll be landing shortly."

Sophie swung her legs off the bed and pushed her fingers through her hair. "I feel uncomfortable in bed. With… a stranger present."

"And that's why I'm here. We must get to know each other so that we aren't uncomfortable in each other's company. We must be convincing."

Shakily she poured herself a glass of water, took a sip, and collected herself and turned to him. "What do you need to know?"

He leaned against the wall of the bedroom. "Your likes, your dislikes. Your temperament, I can guess."

She looked up at him in surprise. She didn't think he'd paid the least bit of attention to her, let alone have an idea as to her temperament.

"Really? You need to know?"

He smiled and waved a piece of paper. "Oh yes I've even been given a list." He held it out to her.

She took it and scanned it. "Any skeletons in the cupboard?" she read out loud. Then looked up at him. "No."

"None whatsoever? Because we will need to know to be prepared."

"No, none."

"Come on, you're beautiful. No boyfriends I should know about?"

"No." She didn't elaborate. Let him simply believe that there were no boyfriends he needed to be aware of. He didn't need to know that there had never been any boyfriends, *ever*.

Besides, who would believe she'd reached the age of twenty-four and was still a virgin?

He raised his eyebrows. "Really?"

"I didn't realize I had to reveal everything to you when I agreed to pretend to be your girlfriend."

"It was not part of the agreement, but it would certainly make the exercise more convincing."

"Exercise?"

"What else would you call it?"

She shrugged.

"Anyway"—he looked at the list—"I know you worked from home as a systems analyst. And you're sure you've had no relationships we need to be aware of?"

She was beginning to feel irritated and met his gaze with a determined one of her own. "Quite."

He tossed away the papers. "A woman of mystery. Okay. You may keep the details to yourself—"

"Thank you." He didn't seem to notice her sarcasm.

"So long as there truly isn't anything I should know. I don't want this whole charade to backfire on me."

She shook her head. "No. I can assure you the journalists would have to have vivid imaginations to make my life interesting."

He frowned slightly, pressed his lips together as if stopping himself from speaking. "So be it. Then we shall agree that we met in Paris at the recent talks and have been inseparable ever since."

"But… the hotel staff will know otherwise."

"They've been paid not to broadcast your work there."

"Oh! I guess that's everything covered then." She slipped her shoes on and stepped toward the door. "So if we've finished I'll get my things together."

"We haven't finished yet." He walked to the bed, picked up a length of silk and came toward her.

She stood before him, chin raised, trying to regulate her breathing, trying to quiet the tremor of attraction which came on every time she was near him. She swallowed and focused on the smooth plane of his cheekbone, not his eyes. She'd be lost if she looked in his eyes.

He touched her hand. "You're shaking. Have I made you so afraid?"

"I'm not afraid."

"Then what is it?" She shook her head and tried to turn away. But he stopped her. "Tell me."

She moved uncomfortably, still focused below his eyes. "I'm not used to…" She was about to continue but he tipped her chin with his finger, so lightly it shouldn't have made her move. But she did. She looked into his eyes and what she saw there robbed her of speech. He was interested in her. And not just interested. His eyes held a restrained sexuality that nearly undid her.

She swallowed again and shook her head. "Please." His face was dark but then the sun suddenly rose and a spark of fire shot through his eyes. She had hardly been aware of how she came to be there but she stood close to him, breathing rapidly, feeling angry at his intrusive questions. But more than that, with every answer, feeling how totally inadequate she was, how out of his league she was. And worst of all, how much she wanted to be in his league. "I can't do this." She turned away from him.

His hands settled briefly before his fingers folded around her arms. She closed her eyes and inhaled.

"Yes, you can. And you will." Did she move to lean against him or did he step closer to her? She couldn't have said. But whichever it was, she found herself supported by his strength, her back touching his chest, his warm breath against her face as she turned to look at him. Slowly he lifted the length of silk and draped it around her shoulders. "A hijab to cover your head when we enter Sumaira." But his touch did little to calm her. He must have mistaken her reaction for fear because he stepped away. "Come, Sophie, it won't be so bad."

She regained her balance and walked to the bed, busying herself, putting on her watch, collecting the things she'd taken off to get into bed. "No, of course not. I'll be fine." She gave him a quick smile before looking around. "I'm Taurus, stubborn. I'm English through and through. I'm tough."

"Now that, I do *not* believe." He opened the door. "It's time for us to prepare for landing."

She walked into the main cabin and took her seat, and focused determinedly on the view of the land outside, bathed in the red glow of a glorious sunrise. She willed him to leave her alone, to seek out his advisers. She sucked in a sharp breath as he took a seat beside her. He ducked his head and followed her gaze out to the unchanging landscape of bleached white stony land, broken only by shifting sands.

"And what do you think of Sumaira?" He indicated the view, the distant jagged mountains that broke the horizon. The other way was flat for as far as the eye could see, the light shimmering on the horizon.

"Sumaira? We're here already?"

"We've been in Sumaira airspace the past half hour. And yet it's another hour until we land. Sumaira is a large country."

She looked down again. "I had no idea..." She trailed off, suddenly embarrassed by her ignorance of this vast country.

He looked at her astutely. "No. I'm sure you didn't. Most people don't. It's a turbulent land, Sophie. A land full of contradictions, riches, and poverty, a... difficult land to rule."

As he looked with a grim face out at the daunting land, she took the opportunity to look at him close too. And for the first time, she felt something more than physical attraction. She actually felt sorry for him.

"And that's what you'll be doing after you've been crowned king."

"Yes. I have two months before the coronation. The coronation which should have seen my elder brother crowned."

"Prince Jaish?"

"You've done your homework. Yes, my brother was groomed to rule but has disappeared into the outback of Australia."

"Without a trace?"

"No. That only happens in stories, I believe. I knew where he was before my father died. But he's not been heard from since. I'm not even sure if he knows he's dead." He shrugged. "However, he'd made it clear when he left that he had no wish to return. My brother and I are not alike," he added, as if this explained everything. Although it did little to enlighten Sophie as to why Malek's brother had chosen to disappear into the Australian Outback.

They watched the land grow ever larger beneath the plane in silence, both lost in their own thoughts. Sophie wondered what Malek thought as he looked at his land so intently. With his face so close to hers, lit by the rosy light that streamed in the small window, Sophie could see him like she'd never seen him before. His skin, not as dark as that of his countrymen, and his eyes, a stunning blue. He was the most handsome man she'd ever seen. But it wasn't that which made her want to incline her head to his. It was something else. It was in the uncompromising line of his jaw, the firm set of his mouth. He was strong, and his strength drew her to him like a moth to a flame. After years of being the strong one, the idea of being in the arms of this man was seductive.

Suddenly Malek turned to her, his blue eyes searching her face as if for answers. "For some reason, I find it easier to talk with you than with my staff. You come without a history of wanting something from me or my country." He studied her face and frowned. "I suppose, despite the little time I've known you, I trust you."

"And you can... trust me, I mean."

"Good. Because I need to." He looked out the window. "Look, we are close to the city now."

Sophie tore her eyes away from him and looked out her window. She could just distinguish the shapes of houses, the same color as the surrounding land. "This is the city?" It wasn't at all how she'd imagined. Where were the glittering towers and broad thoroughfares of Dubai?

Malek gave her a sharp look. "The outskirts. Sumaira's capital city isn't modern, Sophie. Nor"—he sat forward, emphasizing his point—"will it be poor. You see the docks below? They used to be busy, but since our exports dried up, they've lain virtually empty, and unemployment is high, which has led to unrest. But now that the Desert Kings Accord has been signed, we can return to Sumaira with a solid, strong mandate to face the threat from the east and to renegotiate trade deals which will revitalize our country. But this won't happen if people don't have confidence in their king. And this is where you come in."

"Me, posing as your girlfriend?" Despite the fact Sophie knew it to be a charade, just saying the words gave her a thrill of intimacy.

"Yes. I must confess it wasn't my idea. Mohammed worked for my father, in fact he was his best friend from childhood. I rely on his experience and advice. He persuaded me it could work."

Sophie frowned, wondering how much Malek had to be persuaded. Or whether he'd agreed as easily as she had.

"I trust you haven't had a change of heart, Sophie?"

She shot him what she hoped was a reassuring smile. "No, I never go back on my word."

He nodded slowly. "Good. All you have to do is to act the part of an indulged girlfriend." His gaze intensified and she felt it in every part of her body. "I'm assuming you won't find that too onerous?"

"I don't know. I've never been indulged. It doesn't sound as if I have to do a lot."

A smile tugged at his lips. "You'll have to smile. I know you can do that. But you'll have to practice to make your smiles less tentative."

"They're tentative?"

"As if you're not sure they're welcome."

"I guess I'm *not* sure."

"Your smiles *are* welcome, believe me. I have enough grim faces around me, enough obsequious smiles, to make genuine ones most welcome. No matter how fleeting they may be."

Sophie was too busy trying to regulate the rapid beating of her heart to reply.

"And you must be able to shop, of course. But I'm assuming that's no hardship. It seems to be an innate sense in most women I've met."

"Not this woman."

Malek raised an eyebrow in surprise. "You won't have to *go* to the shops; *they* will be brought to you, of course." He narrowed his gaze on her. "You *do* realize you won't be able to leave the palace, don't you?"

This was the first Sophie had heard. "I can't leave the palace? Not even for sightseeing? Not even on my day off?"

He shook his head. "You won't have a day off, Sophie. Not for sightseeing, nor for any reason whatsoever. For the next six months—from now to the coronation and a few months beyond until I have the confidence of the country—you are to be available to me at a moment's notice. When that time is over, you may leave Sumaira and you'll be able to go wherever you want. Can you do that?" he added more gently.

Could she stay in one place, night and day? Of course she could. After all, that was what she'd been doing the past six years. It wasn't like there was any risk of her putting down roots. Okay, it wasn't the freedom she'd been hoping for but she'd agreed, and one look at the approaching city reminded her it was too late to change her mind.

"I'll do what I've agreed to do. I won't back out of the arrangement. You'll have my services for the next six months."

"And then you'll leave with enough money to do whatever you want, *wherever* you want."

He held her gaze as if trying to understand something more than her words. But before he could speak one of his assistants bowed beside them. He held a bag aloft.

"You Royal Highness," he said, bowing once more. "This is from Prime Vizier Mohammed bin Matraf for Miss Brown. Some things she'll need after we land."

As the assistant backed away, Sophie opened the bag. On top of a neatly folded abaya were sunglasses which, glancing out at the unrelenting sun, she could immediately see would be useful.

"To protect yourself from the paparazzi."

"Not the sun?"

"That, too. But any nervousness, any doubt, will be hidden by the glasses."

She took them and slipped them on, glad of the protection they provided, not least from the invasive eyes of this man sitting beside her.

He indicated the abaya. "You already have a hijab to wear over your head and shoulders. But you should also wear this abaya." He glanced at her pantsuit. "The trousers and jacket are fine and respectful of our culture but, in public at least"—

his glance lingered on her hair which fell around her shoulders—"it is best to leave nothing to the imagination."

"Of course."

"You do not mind?"

"No, why should I? It's your country, your culture, and I'm a stranger here."

"My country, my culture..." He returned his gaze to the view that was beginning to change, the buildings growing taller, the adobe buildings now interspersed with more modern towers that glinted in the bright sunlight, as they approached the central city airport. He turned to her with a wry expression on his face that she'd never seen before. "Then why do I feel such a stranger here too?" he added softly.

"Your Royal Highness? It is time to take your seat for landing," said the same obsequious assistant.

"Of course," said Malek crisply, as if regretting his lapse, as if he hadn't uttered those shocking words. He rose and returned to his office. Sophie watched the land grow ever closer and wondered how two strangers could influence the future of a country that appeared so utterly foreign to them both.

As soon as the plane had landed, everyone moved with military precision, reminding Sophie that the country she was about to step out into wasn't like any she'd read about.

The prime vizier clicked his fingers at her. "Come!"

She snapped off her belt, grabbed her bag, and walked over to him.

Everyone else stayed seated while the two of them walked over to the royal suite. "Are you ready, Your Royal Highness?" he asked.

Malek glanced at Sophie and nodded.

"Good. As soon as the doors are open"—the vizier turned to Sophie—"His Royal Highness will move to the top of the steps and pause there for photographs to be taken."

She tried to swallow her fear.

The vizier sighed and shook his head, concerned. He wasn't the only one wondering how on earth she was going to manage. "And then I want you to step up behind him. He'll glance at you and you will follow him. Follow his every move but do *not* step ahead of him."

"Right. Got it."

As he finished speaking, the steps were pushed into place against the plane and secured. The staff stood by, ready for the command to open the doors. She was so nervous she wondered if she'd be able to move at all.

She glanced up at Malek and saw that same slight twitch of muscle in the tight jaw. It seemed she wasn't the only one affected by nerves. He fisted his hands briefly and beckoned to the attendant to open the doors.

A flood of heat and light entered the plane. Sophie nearly recoiled. She slid on the glasses, suddenly thankful for the vizier's thoughtfulness.

The adviser beckoned to Malek who stepped out into the blinding light. It sounded like chaos outside. Cheers and shouts of "Your Royal Highness, this way!" filled the air. Sophie suddenly felt totally out of her depth. Talking it through was one thing; acting it out, in front of a real audience, was entirely another. Suddenly she felt a little push, and she stepped right behind Malek.

"Stand up straight," the vizier hissed. She stood straight, her eyes in a direct line with Malek's broad shoulders. In his robes, he was a different person—transformed into someone exotic and strange. She gripped the hijab, which she'd wrapped around her head and shoulders with the help of an assistant. She could do this.

Then Malek moved and so did she. He took a step down the flight and revealed the chaos below her. She'd have fled if it weren't for the vizier coming up right behind her, his hand firmly pushing her forward.

With her hand holding on to the rail—she didn't want to go flying into Malek's back—she walked as carefully as possible to the tarmac upon which waves of heat shimmered. She tried to contain the impulse to gasp for air. The contrast of the air-conditioned plane to the raw heat of the tarmac was dramatic.

Sophie concentrated on her breathing and focused on Malek, trying to keep at bay the panic that threatened to consume her. I can do this, she said to herself. After six months it'll mean freedom for me. And that's what I wanted, wasn't it? At that moment, Malek stepped to one side, and Sophie was faced with an onslaught of camera flashes, TV cameras pointed at her, and a barrage of questions. For a split second she froze, but then she felt the touch of a hand on her sleeve, and she looked across to Malek. For the first time since she'd met him, she forgot he was royal, about to become king of a large country. He was simply a man, reaching out for her, understanding her panic, and calming her, all with that one touch. But it was more than the touch, it was in his eyes—intimate and sympathetic. Instantly the throng of the press receded from her consciousness. He dipped his head to her. "Are you okay?" he said in a low voice that only she could hear.

She pursed her trembling lips and nodded.

"Good."

They exchanged another complicit glance and he turned, slowly taking his hand from her arm as myriad cameras flashed again. And she suddenly realized why he'd done it. It wasn't because he was concerned for her. It was for the cameras. To let the whole world know that he, Crown Prince

Malek of Sumaira, had a mistress. He was a red-blooded male who wouldn't be marrying anyone so obviously inappropriate, but would be a good catch for any of the daughters of the principal families and tribes of Sumaira.

Malek continued to walk away from the crowds toward the VIP entrance and another timely shove from the vizier had her following close behind.

Soon they were through the formalities of the airport and on the way to the palace. Sophie sat beside Malek while the vizier sat up front with the driver. Malek didn't speak but looked out at his people who lined the road, and waved at them from time to time. Sophie focused her gaze above the people, looking up at the buildings that tumbled on top of each other, as they climbed the hill away from the airport and the sea toward the ridge that rose above the city, along which a massive fortress rose.

Sweat still bloomed on her skin despite the air-conditioned car. She couldn't take her eyes off the fortress which expanded as they grew nearer, into a palace of considerable size that was built over the entire ridge. Her feelings of trepidation grew. She glanced nervously at Malek, who must have sensed her discomfort.

"Wondering what you've let yourself in for?" he said this without looking at her.

"Yes, to be honest. Is that the palace?"

He looked up to the ridge. "Indeed. It started off as a fifth-century fortress."

"And it's now?"

"A twenty-first-century fortress."

"Oh, just the date's changed."

He gave a humorless laugh as the huge gates slid into place behind them. But Sophie didn't laugh. The grinding of the gates as they slid into the stone surrounds sent a shiver down her spine.

CHAPTER 5

"It's not as bad as it looks," Malek said, without looking at her. "Whatever breezes blow in from the sea or from across the mountains are caught on the ridge and make it very unfortress-like."

As they passed through the palace walls, the cheering crowds ended and were replaced with something that Sophie had totally not expected.

"Oh my God, this is beautiful." The trees were green, and lively up here, catching the breeze, just as Malek had described. Small rainbows hung over the fountains where water splashed from ornate stonework into pools that ran from one to another, along rills of aquamarine that marked the ancient white stonework like a grid.

Even the palace buildings, once inside the fortress walls, were beautiful. The windows were arched and large and inviting.

"Nothing much has changed here for centuries. But my ancestors liked their comfort and their luxuries so I doubt you'll find it too rustic."

Sophie couldn't prevent a brief laugh of surprise escaping. Malek obviously had no idea of how ordinary people lived. She tried to turn it into a cough but, judging by Malek's expression, she failed. "I'm sure you're right."

"You'll be shown your suite of rooms. I'll be tied up for the next few hours with meetings, but we'll see each other at dinner."

Sophie suddenly felt panicked again. The only person she knew in this entire country—notwithstanding his vizier—was about to disappear into this vast palace.

He seemed to sense her panic. "The palace can appear like a maze at first, but your personal maid will make sure you don't get lost. She's been instructed to prime you in some of our customs. Listen to her well."

She stepped out of the car in front of a row of shallow steps and watched Malek walk away, surrounded by officials. She looked around to find a maid bowing before her, waiting for her to allow her to stand.

"Please…" said Sophie. "Stand."

The woman smiled. "My name is Raisa."

"And mine is Sophie."

The woman bobbed another nervous curtsey. "Welcome to Sumaira."

Sophie grinned. Despite the high-profile reception, no one had actually welcomed her to this strange country yet. "Thank you. I hope you'll be able to show me around."

The woman nodded uncertainly. "Would you like to go to your rooms?"

The thought of finding solace on her own, in her own space, suddenly became very appealing. "Yes. Thank you."

Malek was right. It was a maze—a maze of echoing tiled hallways, walled gardens, cloistered shadowy walkways supported by ancient columns and carved stone ceilings under which the air was cooler. Now and then Sophie caught a glimpse of the city and the sea beyond one way, and of the mountains the other. The palace was positioned not just for comfort, but to dominate the land around it.

One last twist and turn and Raisa opened a door for Sophie. "Here is your room." Raisa followed Sophie inside, showing her around. "And here is your wardrobe." Raisa couldn't contain her excitement as she opened it for Sophie.

There were dresses, the color and sheen of jewels, feminine pantsuits, and more casual clothes. "Whose are these?"

"They're yours, of course. The prime vizier ordered it."

"But how did you know my size?" she said, as she ran her fingers over the beautiful fabrics.

"He estimated it and told us your coloring, and we took the liberty of getting you a few things. Tomorrow, of course, the people will come and you can choose your own wardrobe. But for tonight"—Raisa plucked one long, satin gown from the wardrobe—"we thought this would be most appropriate."

Sophie took it from Raisa and held it up to the light. The crimson satin gown was the epitome of luxury. "Appropriate, for what?" She looked at the woman, alarmed.

"For the banquet." Raisa walked away. "I'll leave you to rest and will return to help you get ready in a few hours."

As soon as the door closed, Sophie pushed open the french windows and stepped outside into the private courtyard. Sheltered from the drying desert winds on three sides, the fourth side looked out, across the uneven roofline of the city, to the deep azure of the ocean. Brilliant flowering climbers in bright orange, scarlet, and pink framed the view, shifting in the wind, as if trying to get more comfortable.

She breathed deeply of the scented air and tried to figure out how the hell she'd come from poor but free kitchen-hand to this luxury prison in twenty-four hours. She went inside and undressed, and lay looking up at the slowly whirring ceiling fan.

But she knew how she'd come to be here. For the first time in her life she'd been seduced by a handsome man with a compelling mind. As jet lag overcame her and she closed her eyes, her thoughts were of a man whose eyes probed into the depth of her, whose voice caressed her and whose presence made her forget everything she'd ever thought she wanted.

"MADAM." Again the whisper. This time a touch. "It's time."

Sophie groaned as she returned from her seductive dreams and opened her eyes. Her maid, Raisa, stood before her, concern etched onto her face. "I'm sorry, madam, but if you leave it any longer you will be late. And that mustn't happen."

Sophie swung her legs off the bed and tried to shrug off the stuffy headachy feeling that filled her whenever she slept during the day. She stood. "How much time do I have?"

"You only have two hours."

"Two hours?" Sophie laughed. "Right. I'll go and shower and maybe you could…" For the life of her she couldn't think what Raisa was going to do. She waved her hand. "Do whatever it is you think ought to be done."

When Sophie emerged from the shower, she was surprised to see Raisa had followed her into the luxurious marble bathroom.

Sophie grabbed the towel from her. "It's okay. I can sort myself out."

Raisa looked wounded. "But, madam," she began to remonstrate. "I am to help you prepare for tonight." She held up a tray of lotions. "A massage will help you recover from your travels."

Sophie shook her head decisively. "I'll be out in a

moment, and perhaps you'd be so kind as to do my hair for me?" Raisa still looked a little doubtful. "Please indulge my Western ways. I'm not used to such *personal* attention. But I'd appreciate you doing something with my hair."

Raisa inspected her hair as if she were sizing up a problem, and nodded confidently before leaving the bathroom.

Sophie sighed. Somehow she didn't think she was ever going to get used to this.

RAISA GAVE her hair a final twist with the straightening irons, checked to make sure the tiny satin-covered buttons of the dress were fastened securely and stepped away with a nod of satisfaction. "Now you may look."

From shy beginnings, Raisa had quickly become very bossy about Sophie's appearance. Sophie walked over to the mirror and stared at her reflection. Then she frowned and looked away, almost expecting the reflected image to remain unmoving. But the image in the mirror followed her own movements. "Wow!" She swished her hair down her naked back. It tickled her skin, stimulating it in a deliciously sensual way. "You've done an amazing job. I hardly recognize myself!"

"I did very little, madam. You are very beautiful." Raisa came up and stood beside her and met Sophie's gaze in the mirror.

"Are you sure it's okay for me to dress like this?"

"Inside the palace, it is fine to wear Western clothes. But outside you must wear an abaya and the hijab over your head and shoulders. Like this." She draped the matching hijab around Sophie's hair and shoulders. Raisa stood back and smiled approvingly.

Sophie was embarrassed by Raisa's intense scrutiny. "Should I leave now?"

"No, you have half an hour."

"Good. I'll go and get some fresh air. From what you've described, I'll be tied up with formality for the rest of the evening."

"And don't forget, when someone introduces someone to you, you must look down. It's very bad form to look eye-to-eye with someone."

"But that's contrary to the way I was brought up," Sophie protested.

Raisa adjusted the strap of Sophie's new evening gown. "You are not in your country, now, Miss Sophie. You are in Sumaira."

How could she forget? "Thank you. You can leave now."

"I'll wait outside, madam. You'll never find your way on your own."

It made Sophie feel worse. Like some mouse, trapped in a maze. A dressed-up mouse, she thought miserably. But she indicated her agreement before stepping outside into the courtyard.

It was late now. Daylight had suddenly given way to sultry darkness. There was no long twilight as there was in England or France, no imperceptible shifting between day and night. Here, so much nearer to the equator, night fell like the swirl of a star-studded purple cloak, robbing the world of light but gifting it with its own celestial brilliance.

It was not only beautiful, Sophie thought, craning her neck to look up at the stars, but it was also more comfortable. The heat of the day still radiated out from the stonework on the terrace and walls, but the breeze had quickened, moving the warm air, making it easier to breathe, soothing her skin.

She inhaled the scented air and for the first time that day felt she could cope with what lay ahead. After all, hadn't she coped with the worst life could throw at her already? Her mother's tragic illness and death.

She gave a small cry and turned sharply away, as if trying to avoid the memories which were still too recent to be relived without pain. She walked to the fountain and sat on its edge, unable to resist plunging her hand into the water, swirling it back and forth. She disturbed the reflection of stars, watching them shift into new patterns, as she tried in vain to hold in the tears that distorted the light still further.

Her mother would be proud of her, she insisted to herself. She was doing what she'd always wanted to do—traveling and experiencing new things. She looked up into the sky once more. She'd heard once that you couldn't cry looking upwards. Her hand stilled on the water, fingers spread out as if soothing the water back to its reflective state. She sighed once more. It seemed to work. The tears had gone and, when she looked at the water, the stars reflected their full glory at her.

Then she looked up suddenly. What was that? She froze, listening intently. She'd imagined this courtyard was private. But now, as she looked more closely through the tracery of green, she could see a light coming from the far side. She rose silently. Her skin prickled. She felt as if she were being watched. Was she? Had someone witnessed her tears? She panicked at the thought. She never broke down in public. Her feelings, her hurts, were her own—not to be shared. She didn't want pity.

She walked silently toward the light, the only sound the swish of her satin gown against the paving stones. She pushed aside a swath of heavy flowering creepers and looked to the far building. The windows were open—an oversized lamp beside a settee was the source of the light. It was someone's living room. But whose? She was curious and stepped forward, wondering if it were an office, or her maid's quarters, wanting to know whose rooms were so close to her own.

It wasn't until she'd walked up to the open doors that she smelled the blend of aromas. She knew whose room it was. There was no mistaking the strong coffee overlaid with the masculine aftershave with notes of ambergris and leather. The smell curled inside her and tugged.

"Sophie?"

Sophie spun around. Malek stood in the shadows of the overhanging trees, dressed in a dinner suit, his expression unreadable in the darkness.

"Expecting someone else? You have any other English girls stashed away up here?"

He stepped out from the shadows. "No, I don't have many English girls stashed away at the moment." He paused, his eyes taking her in. "You've been well attended? Everything has been to your satisfaction?"

She nodded. "Everyone has been very attentive. But mostly I slept. Raisa is going to take me to the reception shortly."

"Ah, the reception. It will be dull, no doubt, but it'll be an opportunity for you to appear by my side at a state reception."

"Is there anything I need to know?"

"Avoid mentioning your work for us at the hotel. It's not a disaster if you do, but it will look better if you stick to the story my prime vizier has created."

"Sure." Sophie looked away. She hated deceit.

"Sophie?"

She turned to face him. He was closer than she imagined, his gaze warmer than she'd seen it before. He took a step closer still, and she could have sworn she stopped breathing.

"You look beautiful." His voice was soft, wondering almost, and she felt the vicious lick of desire deep within.

Instinctively she opened her mouth to deny his words but a sharp rap on the door broke the moment, and the prime vizier stepped into the courtyard.

Malek frowned. "Mohammed! Did you want something?"

Prime Vizier Mohammed clasped his hands and bowed his head, but when he stood tall, Sophie could see in his eyes that he didn't consider himself subservient in any way. "Miss Brown should return to her room, Your Royal Highness. Her servant is becoming anxious. She should proceed to the reception shortly."

Malek grimaced, obviously irritated by the interruption. "He's right, Sophie. You should go."

"Of course." She walked away and then, remembering herself, stopped, and gave some sort of bow which she hoped would satisfy them both. But judging by Malek's wry smile and the vizier's frown, she somehow doubted it.

She picked up her long gown and walked quickly away to her room. Only when she reached its open doors did she stop and look back. She couldn't see either Malek or the vizier now, but she could hear their footfalls as they walked toward Malek's room and the sonorous tones of the vizier. Briefly, she wondered what would have happened if the vizier hadn't arrived at that moment. Then she heard Malek's deep voice speak to his vizier before they retreated into his room, and she forgot everything except how his voice made her feel.

Feminine. Utterly feminine. His voice curled its way deep inside her and set her heart racing and her sex throbbing. She seemed preternaturally aware of his presence. Even when she couldn't see him, every sense in her body vibrated with an acute awareness of him. She wanted him, in the most primitive way possible. And although she couldn't have him, she couldn't stop herself from looking forward to seeing him again.

She stepped inside her room and Raisa immediately descended on her with a make-up brush and perfume spray, no doubt scolding her in her own language. But Sophie didn't listen—she was thinking of Malek. She wouldn't be in Sumaira for long. She wouldn't be in Malek's presence for long. But while she was there, she could enjoy it—enjoy *him*. Because like it or not, she was irrevocably attracted to him.

"AND YOU'RE FROM?"

Sophie tore her gaze from Malek who was seated a little way along the table from her. They'd had no opportunity to talk but she'd been aware of his every move, of his every glance toward her. And so, it would seem, had everyone else.

She turned to the person who'd asked the question—sheikh and leader of Sumaira's dominant Bedouin tribe—the Boqom.

"England," she replied. She saw Malek move, alert to her reply, and smiled to herself.

The old sheikh nodded. "Now *that* much I had gathered."

"The Cotswolds in south central England. Have you been there?"

"No. I've been to London, of course, and Oxford to visit friends. But not the Cotswolds. And… you met His Royal Highness there?"

She shook her head and frowned, hoping she didn't say the wrong thing. "No, in Paris."

"Hm," the old man said thoughtfully, looking at her intently. "And you two are…" He paused, as he obviously tried to find a polite way of asking. He shrugged, having given up. "Are together?"

Sophie blushed. "I, well, it's…" she stammered.

"I'm sorry. I was indelicate. Of course, you can't—and

shouldn't—say. It's just that your presence has aroused the curiosity of everyone present here. Malek, himself, has always been an enigma. He's not like his father who never hid his love of women. And he's not like his elder brother who was very much like his father. You must understand that such machismo is admired in our country."

Sophie acknowledged his words, eyes firmly focused on her plate of half-eaten delicacies. She pressed her lips together. She was determined not to say anything in case it was the wrong thing. Not that the old sheikh appeared concerned by her silence. He was obviously used to women being seen and not heard. He was gazing at Malek.

"Hm." He looked back at her and smiled. "I apologize for being indelicate. Now, tell me about these... Cotswolds. Is it pleasant there?"

Sophie was relieved to be able to talk about something she knew about. She had no idea what political machinations she was a part of but she was on safe ground talking about her old home.

"Very. If you imagine a chocolate-box picture of England, all thatched cottages, Georgian manor houses, and medieval churches."

"And you lived in such a manor house?"

Sophie nearly choked on her water. She shook her head. "No. My home is nothing like that!"

"Sophie is nothing if not modest about her upbringing."

Both she and the old sheikh turned around in surprise to see Malek standing behind them, one hand proprietorially gripping her chair.

"Malek!" exclaimed the old man. "This charming young lady was telling me about her home."

Malek glanced at Sophie. "And being characteristically modest about it, too, from what I heard."

"Very laudable," the old man responded. "If only my own daughters had such modesty."

A smile tugged at Malek's lips. It was obviously the understatement of the year.

"But my granddaughter, Your Royal Highness, has been brought up well by her tutors," continued the old sheikh.

"Shamma?"

"Indeed. My eldest granddaughter is eighteen now," he said, his eyes narrowing as he looked at Malek intently. "And of marriageable age," he added, as if his meaning hadn't been quite clear.

Malek nodded, his face becoming inscrutable once more. "And she's studying, I understand?"

"In Paris at the moment. But is due here for the coronation. If not before."

Sophie made a mental note to check the files on who this girl might be. Whether she was a front runner or not. Her grandfather obviously considered she was. Then she looked at the old sheikh. He'd appeared pleasant enough. But then, she was rapidly learning, nothing was at it appeared in Sumaira.

Malek sat and the old sheikh continued to talk leaving Sophie to sit and watch… and daydream.

MALEK STAYED SEATED between Sophie and the old sheikh the rest of the evening, obviously wanting to add fuel to the gossip. His presence also had the added advantage that he could guide the conversation so Sophie couldn't incriminate them. She should have felt used, but how could she when Malek's presence had such a pleasurable effect on her? It was like someone was breathing on her neck, or nibbling her ear —just being near him sent skitters of delight flowing through her. And while her body responded to his proximity, she listened to his stories of the high-profile personalities with whom he'd been involved as an international lawyer, working on some of the most significant cases of the decade. He was clever. He moved between entertaining anecdotes and serious ideas with ease, avoiding contentious topics, treading carefully. He might not have wanted to rule, thought Sophie, but he was a consummate politician, all the same.

It was midnight before the dinner concluded. They all walked out together into the foyer to farewell their guests. From the foyer, a private balcony looked out onto the circular drive and a gated area which had been set up for journalists, within the high external walls of the castle.

Malek walked up to the doors and looked back at her. "Sophie! Come, they will want to see you, too."

The prime vizier motioned encouragingly. "You will need to wear your hijab."

Sophie placed the long length of silk over her head and around her bare shoulders and the vizier smiled approvingly.

She walked over to Malek and paused uncertainly. He put his hand on her waist and urged her forward. As they both emerged and waved to the departing guests, there were shouts and camera flashes from the gated area.

It was unreal. The lights and clamor of the journalists, the heat and fragrance of the night drifting up to the balcony from below. It was light years away from anything she'd ever been used to and she trembled under the intense gaze of the crowds.

Malek dipped his head to her. "Are you okay?" he murmured, his fingers fanning out on her back in a brief caress which distracted her from her nerves immediately.

She half-turned and smiled. "Kind of. This is like nothing I've ever done before."

"It doesn't show. You look beautiful and poised. You're a

natural." Again, another brief caress which made Sophie *feel* very natural. "Only one thing missing." His breath was hot against her neck and she involuntarily arched against him.

"Hm?" was all she could say.

"You need to wave, Sophie."

"Wave?" She looked up at him, the spell broken. "Why would they want me, of all people, to wave to them?"

"Because you're with me, and you're beautiful. Those are sufficient reasons."

Her mind stopped on "beautiful" and hesitantly she raised her hand. She didn't wave it back and forth, simply raised it and immediately cameras flashed across the dark night, making her blink and step back... back against Malek's strong body.

Startled she went to move away but he raised his hand and placed it on her upper arm and inclined his head toward hers as if to whisper something seductive. His gaze never left the photographers. "Your smile has disappeared. Give them another one, another wave, give them what they want and they'll leave."

She willed her confusion to turn into a smile and she looked at the cameras. Another clatter of shutter sounds greeted her glance.

"You have your shots," said the vizier, stepping forward to address the crowd. "So now, please allow His Royal Highness and"—he glanced at Sophie—"Miss Brown to finish their evening in peace."

The vizier motioned to security who stepped forward to escort the host of photographers and journalists out of the palace grounds.

Malek and Sophie withdrew into the palace foyer. He stopped under the shadows of an archway. "You've done well tonight. It can't have been easy."

Sophie thought for a moment and looked up at him, his

face shadowed, not the crown prince now. "Easy? No. It felt surreal. But it wasn't hard either. Not with…" She stopped herself just in time. She wasn't used to censoring what she said. So many years on her own, she'd never had to make sure she said the right thing, made the right noises, played any game other than her own. But now she did.

His eyes held hers. "Not with?" he prompted. "What were you about to say?" His words were low, meant for her alone. She felt them like a caress, and it released her caution.

"Not with you beside me."

His expression didn't change. He tilted his head to one side as if trying to work her out. "Good," he whispered, his lips opening softly.

She licked her own lips.

"Your Royal Highness," the prime vizier called. Malek sighed and turned away from Sophie.

"Yes?"

Sophie leaned against one of the pillars that rose into the lofty heights of the foyer and watched as Malek listened to his adviser talk to him. She should go. Return to her room. But even if she knew the way, she needed time to recover. Her heart was racing and her legs felt weak. Seeing Malek talk to his adviser, he was the all-powerful ruler of Sumaira once more, and she wondered how on earth the intimacy of the past few moments had happened. Then the vizier left. Malek raked his fingers through his short hair, twisted around, and caught her gaze.

This was madness. She pushed herself off the pillar. She had to get away. She opened the nearest door but was met by a turning of heads as staff looked at her with curiosity.

"Sorry!" she said quickly closing the door.

"Sophie, this way," said Malek, as he opened a door for her.

She took a deep breath and walked over to him, unable to look him in the eye.

"Are you okay?" he asked.

"Just tired."

"I'm not surprised. Much has happened in the past few days." He opened the door and stepped back. "After you."

She looked around for her maid. "I'll ask Raisa to take me to my room."

"There's no need. I'll walk you there."

They walked in silence along a deserted corridor that Sophie vaguely recognized. Moonlight pooled through the high windows, making the white marble gleam. It was something out of a fairy tale. Then Malek stopped suddenly. "We'll take a shortcut through the gardens."

Within moments, Sophie could see why. These gardens were on a more ancient side of the palace and had a wilder appearance. The climbers grew around the pillars with abandon and with minimal interference from the gardeners. The result was lush and sensuous.

"It's beautiful here." Sophie was drawn toward an open view of the city, framed by the rampant growth. "How come it's been left so wild?"

Malek nodded toward a flat-roofed building which opened onto the garden. "That was my grandmother's suite. She appreciated nature and insisted her gardens be kept like this. She died recently, and I haven't had the heart to change anything yet."

Those words drew Sophie's gaze to his face for the first time since they'd left the Great Hall. It was like a small window had opened onto his soul, something real, something hidden, and something she could relate to.

"You miss her."

He smiled. "She was closer to me than my own parents. They were always too busy with politics, with goading each other, with hurting each other, to pay much attention to their second son."

"That's a shame. It must have been hard for you growing up."

He glanced at her. "No. I didn't miss them. I was glad I was out of it. My brother was always at the center of everything, whether he liked it or not. And most of the time, he didn't."

"Maybe that's why he left."

Malek glanced at her sharply before returning his gaze to the view. The silence lengthened and Sophie began to regret speaking her mind.

"I'm sorry," she said. "I'm probably wrong. It's just that I could imagine that someone... with that amount of pressure, might simply want to get away."

Malek leaned against a pillar and looked directly at her. She struggled to remain still under his intense gaze. "No need to apologize, Sophie. You're right. Of course, you're right. I haven't wanted to admit it to myself; I've been too busy feeling angry with him. But he had to get away."

"Is he coming home?"

Malek shook his head. "I don't know. I've only spoken with him once and that didn't go well. No. Our country can't wait to see if he changes his mind. I have to get on with things, assuming he's gone for good." He leaned against the stone parapet and looked out across the city toward the sea. "But, you know, in some ways, I'm glad I've returned. I've spent too long away. I'd forgotten..."

Sophie was curious. Malek's face held a faraway look as he looked out across the city lights to the inky black of the sea.

"What had you forgotten?"

He was silent for a few moments. "The smell of the land.

It's in my bones, and I almost forgot it. And the colors. See…"
He beckoned her to step in front of him.

She did as he bade and looked out, down the sightline of
his finger. "You see here…"

"The flashing light?"

"Yes, the lighthouse. It was a constant beacon in my life,
growing up. I could see it from here, the city palace, and
from the mountain palace where I spent much of my youth.
It connected my two worlds." He paused. "I used to weave
tales around it. It was a lifeline of sorts." He shrugged and
sighed. "I suppose you think this is crazy talk coming from a
member of the royal family."

"Everyone needs a lifeline from time to time. Everyone
has some kind of lighthouse in their life. Even kings."

He smiled. "Even kings," he repeated softly.

Their faces were close, and when he raised his hand to
her cheek she began to move away. This was crazy. How the
hell had she let this happen? Then he looked away suddenly,
and his mouth hardened into a line. "I'm sorry. I'd thought
tonight's photo session would be sufficient. But it appears
some hardened paparazzi are lurking on the nearby
rooftops."

She turned to look, fully expecting to see cameras trained
on her. "I don't see—"

"You won't. I know this view like the back of my hand.
The city lights never glint on the adobe roofs… not unless
there are cameras with zoom lenses on them. And there are
tonight."

"But that's terrible. Aren't you allowed any privacy?"

"Of course not. Not now I will be king." He searched her
eyes with compassion. "I'm sorry, Sophie. But you're in this
now. I hope you understand. Please… stay where you are…
give them time. They loved you. And they will appreciate
these photos of us together. They will be able to sell them at

great profit. It'll work for them. And it'll work for us. So stay... please."

She couldn't have moved even if she'd wanted to. The expression in his eyes robbed her of thought and movement. He shifted her hair off her shoulder, gathering it into one hand and draping it over her other shoulder. "You smell beautiful."

"You don't have to say that for the camera," she murmured. "Not unless it has a long-distance microphone, too." She felt his smile as his lips touched her neck and she gasped as she tilted her head against her shoulder. She swallowed. "You really want them to have a convincing photo this time, don't you?"

He slid his hand around her waist and pulled her against his body. She gasped again as she felt his erection hard against her back. "Some things, the camera won't see. Some things," he murmured against her cheek, "only you will know."

She should have cried out. She should have gone running there and then. She hadn't signed up for this.

He pulled away. "But don't worry. This isn't something I'm going to act on. I can't help myself. You're a beautiful and alluring woman. I'd have to be made of stone not to be affected by you."

She was trembling from head to foot. She twisted in his arms. "I can't do this anymore. No more tonight, anyway."

He nodded. "I'm sorry. I tried to prepare you earlier, to tell you that we would be beginning the charade this evening, but we were interrupted. And I hadn't anticipated that I, that we..."

"I need to return to my room," she said quickly.

"Of course. I'll take you there."

They left the openness of the terrace and retreated into the labyrinthine walls of the palace. It was dark and shadowy under the colonnaded walkways. She was aware of him, of his every movement, of every sound of his footfall and the swish of her satin gown on the old stonework. They reached her room too quickly. She looked up into his still curious gaze.

"Thank you for taking me to my room. I could have called Raisa, you know."

"I know."

She hardly dared to breathe, wondering whether he was thinking the same as her. She could barely distinguish his features in the dark of the courtyard.

"But it was no trouble." He smiled. "Goodnight."

She sucked in another sharp breath as he stepped toward her... and then past her, before turning toward his own room.

He didn't look back at her. She opened her door and stepped inside. Of course he wouldn't look back. Why would he? For all the intimacy, he was still the crown prince and out of her reach.

She closed her door behind her and sank against it, shutting her eyes. She was wildly attracted to this man who was as different to her as the stars. But she couldn't just walk away. She had to work with him... and she had to pretend they were the lovers that they could never be.

CHAPTER 6

*T*he first weeks passed in a whirl of work and formal dinner engagements. The mornings were spent in the office working on the tasks which Malek had set her, in meetings with the king's advisers, and generally getting to grips with the palace's outdated IT systems for which Sophie already had new ideas. The job she disliked the most was researching and narrowing the long list of women who would make a suitable queen for Malek. *That* she always had least time for.

It was the afternoons and evenings she lived for. From that moment after lunch when she would receive the call from Malek's office to attend him, her heart beat a little bit faster.

She didn't know where they were going from one day to the next. One day they would be attending the opening of the new wing of the university, she—some distance behind him —a part of the company, but not so close as to be improper. The next day they could be at a formal luncheon, given by one of the many groups intent on influencing the man who would shortly be their king. Again, Sophie would be seated at a little distance from Malek, for proprietary's sake, but still everyone knew that she was there for, and with, Malek.

During these occasions, she would talk politely with the other guests and watch Malek. She was becoming accustomed to every nuance of his expression. From the slight narrowing of the eyes when he was displeased, to the barely perceptible twitch at the corners of his mouth when something amused him. But whatever might be going on inside him, he was always fair, diplomatic, and watchful. He was a man under siege, but he never let it show.

At least not in company. Only with her, in the evenings, when after that first night he would make sure they had time alone, no matter which function they had to attend. It was these moments, when darkness surrounded them in their private courtyard, where the table would be laid with food and drinks, that she enjoyed the most. There was no repetition of the physical intimacy of their first night together. They would simply talk and relax.

And tonight was no different. As Malek passed Sophie a small glass of herb tea and she sat amidst the cushions, she experienced a sense of relief that the work and formality of the day had ended, and that they had a time of quiet respite together. Two people who both, for different reasons, felt like misfits in this strange country.

As he held up his glass to hers he smiled. Not a tugging at the lips, but a full smile that lit his face, creating warmth, low in her stomach. He had gotten to her and there was nothing she could do about it. She'd fallen for him, despite her caution. She put down her glass and sighed.

"Why the big sigh, Sophie?"

It seemed he was getting to know her too. She shrugged. "Just been a long day I guess. Constantly under the public eye. I'm not used to it."

Malek took a sip from his glass and considered her. "A

long few weeks too. I'm sorry, I know you're accustomed to your independence, but you can't leave the palace by yourself, unfortunately. As I've explained, unemployment is high, there have been incidents... and I cannot guarantee your safety."

"It's okay. I thought I'd feel trapped, but I haven't. I guess I'm enjoying what I'm doing."

"Then why the sigh?"

She shook her head. "Nothing really."

"I think you know you can trust me by now, Sophie."

How could she tell him that she was sad that her time with him was passing and that she'd soon be gone and he'd be king, engaged to be married to some stranger?

"Tell me," he repeated.

The way he commanded her to speak emphasized the fact that he would shortly be king and she was his subject, and that it would always be that way. She shook her head and focused on taking another sip of her drink. "No. I'd rather not."

But rather than take offense, when she glanced at Malek his lips were quirked into that semi-smile of his. "I apologize. I've obviously become too used to talking with people who respond best to orders. I will ask again. Please, tell me what's troubling you." He rose from the table and walked around to her.

Placing the glass onto the table without revealing her shaking hand was a challenge. A challenge she feared she'd lost when she looked up and saw Malek's gaze follow her trembling hand. Then he looked into her eyes and she knew it was she who was lost.

He took her hand in both of his and swept his thumb over its back, his gaze tracing the movement of his fingers over her skin. Sophie closed her eyes and sucked in a sharp breath, trying to control the instant fire that leaped into being deep inside at the feel of his hand against hers. When she opened them again she saw a new expression in his face. "Sophie," he said with a whisper. "I believe I know what it is you're thinking."

"And how would you know that?" said Sophie in a husky, sultry voice she hardly recognized as her own.

"Because I'm thinking the same."

"I… I doubt that." It would be impossible. For how could Malek, about to be king of such a powerful nation, feel a fraction of what she felt for him?

"There is only one way to find out. Tell me, when I enter my office do you know the first thing I look for?"

"Your coffee?"

"Sophie," Malek warned. "Try again."

"How can I? I can't presume to know the mind of the crown prince."

"But you *can* presume to know the mind of a man."

"Ah, that's quite a different thing. But still I'm not sure I'm any better at knowing the mind of a man, than the mind of the crown prince."

"Try."

Another command. But there was no way out other than to respond. "You look for something, or someone, you need to get you through the day." She looked up suddenly into his eyes that had grown wider with surprise. She'd nailed it. It gave her confidence. "Something or someone who reminds you of life outside of duty." She licked her lips. Should she go on? "Is it a thing or a person?"

"*You.* You know it's you."

She shook her head in disbelief.

"You must have realized. I will be in a meeting with my advisers, they will be squabbling like children over what needs to be done for the monarchy, the country, for diplomacy with our neighbors. There is dissension everywhere.

Some days I feel I'm drowning in it. And then I see you out of the corner of my eye as you pass by and it's as if a gentle breeze has blown into the room and put everything into perspective. I take a deep breath as I try to inhale your perfume, filling myself with your calm, and then you're gone. But you're still with me, and I can go on."

"And when I'm working with the others," said Sophie. "Trying to make sense of the disorder, trying to ignore the heat of the day, and the chaos of voices all around, I see you, and I know I can cope."

Malek lifted her hands to his lips and kissed them gently. He brushed his lips against her skin and looked into her eyes. She wanted her lips to replace her hands. She wanted him pressed against her, wanted his lips on hers, wanted to entwine her arms around him and never let go. Could she? Could she forget they had no future and live in the present and make her dreams a reality? Could she tell him how she felt? All it would take was one sign from him.

"Sophie," he breathed against her skin. "These past weeks have been made bearable only by you. And for that I thank you from the bottom of my heart."

Sophie's heart sank. He was grateful, that was all. She pulled her hand away from his and tried to ignore the fleeting look of hurt in his eyes. "You're welcome. You're paying me well for it." It pained her to see the shutter come over his face. But she had no choice. She felt things for him which weren't and could never be reciprocated. She had to survive, she had to protect herself.

"Of course." His ambiguous response could have meant many things. But from the look in his eye she saw he understood.

"Next week we must begin the process of selecting your new wife."

"My new wife," Malek said, with a bitterness which

soured the atmosphere. He pulled away and walked across to the courtyard and stood looking over the city lights, hands thrust into his pockets. His white shirt gleamed in the dull light. "What the hell have I got myself into, eh, Sophie? A country I haven't lived in for a dozen years, a family I distanced myself from years ago, people who distrust me at best, and hate me at worst, and a marriage built on nothing but politics."

The shreds of self-protection Sophie had been trying to hold on to dissolved instantly as she witnessed his deep sense of helplessness and frustration. She went over to him and touched him on his shoulder. He twisted around instantly as if electrified. He gripped her hand and looked at her urgently.

"How can I do this, Sophie? How can I pretend to be this person I am not?"

She shook her head. "You can't pretend, Malek. But you can be the man you are. That man is more than ready to be king. And when you show that man to the world, they will love you and they will respect you, and you can be the king you want to be."

He drew her gently to him. His palms were warm against the small of her back. "Sophie," he murmured, just before he kissed her.

The kiss was nothing like Sophie had imagined during those long hot nights lying awake thinking of Malek. She could not have conceived how the intensity of his personality could have been so vividly expressed in the kiss; she could not have imagined how that intensity could have been tempered with a sensitivity that called to the very heart of her, unleashing her passion more effectively than any demands could have done.

The kiss grew more passionate as his tongue flicked over her lips, which she parted to allow him greater access. She groaned as he pulled her close against his hard body. The feel of his hand moving under her top against her heated skin only increased her need. With his other hand he thrust his fingers through her hair to tilt her head. She closed her eyes as his mouth moved from her head to her throat and lower.

A sudden flash of light made them both freeze.

"What the hell?" muttered Malek. There was another tell-tale flash of light. He muttered an expletive and tugged her top back over her exposed skin. He took her hand and pulled her away, into the privacy of their courtyard. "Damn, what the hell was I thinking?"

"Neither of us were thinking," Sophie said, as she adjusted her clothing. "Paparazzi?"

He sighed. "Without a doubt. What the hell have I done?" he repeated. "Flirtation is one thing, but that was an entirely different matter." He glanced at her. "I'm sorry, Sophie, I didn't mean to drag your name through the mud."

She gave an uncertain laugh. "Mud? It was a kiss. I think it would take more than a kiss to drag my name through the mud."

"You don't understand. They've been waiting for something like this. Waiting for me to lose control. And I very nearly did. I'm sorry." He looked around, agitated. "You should go."

She nodded. But didn't move. Was their intimacy to end like this?

"Goodnight," he said, as he stepped from her as if she could hurt him. She choked back a response and practically ran into her room, not stopping until she was inside with the door closed. She pulled the white silk curtains together and sat on her bed, looking blindly at the curtains, as if she could see through them, as if she could see Malek, still standing in the courtyard looking at her with that expression in his eyes that made her melt inside. But he wouldn't be. That moment had passed, shot dead by the flash of the paparazzi's camera.

She tried to regulate her breathing but, with the doors, windows, and curtains closed tight, she felt she couldn't breathe, despite the air conditioning. She felt claustrophobic without the sense that Malek was with her, aware of her, wanting her.

But it wasn't to be. He'd made that clear. Whatever he wanted, whatever he felt, they had no future together. Sophie crawled onto her bed without undressing and closed her eyes and held close the memory of his kiss, knowing it would be all she had of Malek to hold on to after she left Sumaira.

THE NEXT MORNING when Malek entered his office he was met by his vizier who was wearing a deep frown on his grizzled face. "Your Royal Highness," he said with a bow. But it didn't fool Malek. He knew when Mohammed wasn't happy.

He sighed and sat. "What is it?"

The old man pointed to the computer screen. "*These. Photos.*" Anger dwelt in each heavily inflected syllable. "What—"

"Was I thinking?" Malek replied, as he sat at his desk to take a closer look. "I think that's pretty obvious. It would be clear to anyone looking at these photos that His Royal Highness Crown Prince Malek of Sumaira was about to make love to a beautiful woman."

"The photos are everywhere," the vizier said coldly.

Malek sighed and scrolled through photo after photo in an almost stop-frame sequence of their mouths growing closer, of his hands under her clothing. What Malek paused on wasn't his own loss of control, but Sophie's. She looked absolutely beautiful and stunningly sexy. He held her in his arms as if she needed support, her head with its mussed hair, resting on his hand as he plundered—it was the only word that would adequately describe what he was doing—her mouth. And her hips, tilted to his in an obvious pose of sexual readiness. Malek raised his eyes to his vizier. "More of the same. I thought this was the plan. What's the problem?" He knew what the problem was, but he wanted to hear it from his adviser.

"Your people want to see a dignified crown prince, enjoying the company of beautiful women, not losing control, not about to have sex with them. That, Your Royal Highness, is inappropriate."

"It was a kiss, Mohammed. Just a kiss. Something people do around the world. Why, even *you* may have done it at some point or other," he added dryly.

His adviser glared at him angrily, slipping into their old relationship of tutor and student. "Don't trivialize this, Malek." He walked across to the window from where he could see the office in which Sophie was working. "Miss Brown is very charming, very intelligent, very beautiful. There's no doubt about any of those things." He turned suddenly and eyeballed Malek. "But she's not Sumairan, so don't get carried away."

Malek rose and strode around the room, suddenly angered by the reminder that he'd never again be free. "As if I could ever do that! I've done everything you've said, Mohammed. I've given up everything for this country. Am I not allowed some fun in the process?"

"The purpose of this exercise is to confirm your status as an eligible, heterosexual bachelor. Unlike your brother, your discretion has meant people haven't seen you with a woman. *That* is all we are rectifying. If only you'd been more like your brother…"

"More like my brother?" Malek retorted angrily. "You mean like the way he left this country in the lurch?"

"You know I don't mean that. We go back a long way, Malek, and I hope I can speak my mind with you."

"And your mind says I should be more like my brother, beloved of everyone it would seem, despite the fact he abandoned us."

The adviser held out his hands, placatingly. "All I mean is that if you'd had high-profile relationships, we wouldn't have to do this."

"As you very well know, I've had one serious, long-term relationship and because of who she is we had to be discreet. She couldn't be tainted by scandal. And I've had to give her up because of all of this." Malek swept his hand around the room, indicating the piles of papers, the computer screens, the list of people he had to see that day.

"Can we publicize it now?"

"No. It's complicated."

"I'm sure it is."

Malek's mood darkened at his adviser's implication. "I'm sure you know who it is. Your spies are everywhere. They'd have told you."

His adviser gave him an enigmatic smile. "Anyway," he continued smoothly. "Simply remember it's for a purpose. Miss Brown never can be, and never will be anything more than a smokescreen for the papers." He bowed superficially and backed out of the room. He hesitated at the door. "In public anyway." Before Malek could respond he'd gone.

Malek knew what he was saying. *Do whatever you like so long as no one knows and you don't get carried away. It is what it is and nothing more.*

Malek looked through the window to where Sophie was working and sighed. Pretending they were lovers had been okay in theory, before he'd gotten to know her better and realized how attracted to her he was. Now the thought of using her in this way disgusted him. He'd never pretended, never done anything underhand in his life before. He'd given up much to become king, but he'd be damned if he'd continue to use Sophie like this. She might appear cool, professional, and able to handle anything, but there was a vulnerability about her he refused to exploit.

The photos from the previous day would have to suffice. He couldn't do this anymore. Besides, he needed her skills to put the antiquated systems he'd inherited from his father. His was a country living in a modern world—like it or not—and its stability and prosperity depended on information, depended on his being in touch with what was going on. Not being insulated from everything as his father had been. He needed to *know* everything. To be one step ahead of his political opponents. And he needed someone of Sophie's exceptional skills to help him.

He turned to his assistant. "Tell Miss Brown to come to my office."

SOPHIE GATHERED her papers and knocked on Malek's door.

"Come!"

Sophie walked inside, the smile on her lips dying as soon as she saw Malek—grim-faced and on the phone. She cleared her throat, keeping her laptop defensively close to her chest, and walked to her usual chair and slid the laptop onto the desk. And waited, trying to balance the intimacy of the night before with the professional distance of that moment.

"Just get them." Malek frowned as he finished his call. He looked up at her but the frown didn't lessen, although the fierce expression in his eyes did. "Sit, please," he added as an afterthought.

She sat on the edge of the hard-backed chair and waited,

thoroughly aware that it wasn't Malek before her, but the crown prince.

He looked at her from beneath a lowered brow, looked at her in a way that was a million miles from how he'd looked at her last night. "Our arrangement, Sophie, it will stop immediately."

She swallowed, buying time to recover from his words. "But..." Sophie frowned. "I don't understand. You mean you want me to leave?"

"No, that isn't what I mean. Your work here, in the office, will continue. That is your place. I need you to improve my systems. And..." He paused as if trying to find the right words. "And I still need you to find me a wife." As he said the last word his cold expression cracked a little. Only a small amount, but enough for Sophie to understand what he was doing.

"Oh. So the girlfriend thing, *that* has to stop."

He pursed his lips together briefly and nodded.

"So... the mission has been accomplished. You've got the photos you want. Job done?"

"Job *overdone*. Last night's photos, well, we went too far. *I* went too far."

"Oh, I see." He regretted it. She was shocked at how bereft she felt. He might want the arrangement to end, but she'd spent all last night going over every detail of her time with Malek, reliving how he made her feel. Imagining what might happen the next time they met. She looked at her hands in her lap, frowning as she tried to focus on anything other than the deep hurt and disappointment that flooded her.

Malek jumped up out of his chair. "I'm not sure you do. It's nothing to do with you. Nothing you've done, or not done. I just feel..." He lifted the blinds in his office, looking out across the palace grounds. Then he let them fall with a snap. "I just feel it's not appropriate. It's..."

"Yes?"

"My country needs reassurance that I can bring stability and tradition to its leadership. I have no option but to think of that first." He cleared his throat. "We need to keep our distance from each other from now on. You will continue your work on the computer systems within the palace and…" He trailed off.

"Nothing more personal than that," said Sophie in a flat voice.

"Indeed. So… is that…" Again, he trailed off with uncharacteristic uncertainty.

"That's absolutely fine," she said between gritted teeth, trying to rein in her anger, which, for the moment, masked her feelings of loss. He obviously hadn't listened to a word she'd said the previous evening. He'd reverted to this cardboard cut-out of a monarch. She felt anger surge inside. "Is that all?"

"Yes."

The room was hot, the whir of the overhead fans seemed to do nothing to stir the air. She had to get out of there. She rose and grabbed her laptop.

"One more thing, Sophie."

She stopped but didn't turn around.

"Find me a wife. Fast. I need the final list of candidates on my desk by tomorrow morning."

"*Candidates?*" She took a deep breath, but it did nothing to control the tumult of emotions. She turned around slowly. "*Candidates?*" she repeated. "You mean the list of women you wish to consider to marry?"

"Yes, of course."

Something in her broke. "Malek! You talk of a *wife* as a candidate, you *hate* your mother, and you're cutting the one real thing that has touched you stone dead, before it has a chance to live. And that's fine. Believe me, I have other priorities too. But…" She paused, stopped by the cold look in his eyes. She closed her own eyes against the cold and remembered the heat of his passion the night before. It gave her the courage to continue, the courage to tell the truth. "But," she repeated more firmly, opening her eyes once more. "You can't keep doing this." She bit her lip. This was ridiculous, who was she to lecture the crown prince? "I'm sorry, I'll—"

"Doing what?" One look at Malek and she could see he was genuinely puzzled.

"You really don't know?"

"No, otherwise I wouldn't have asked."

"You're pushing away anything, *anyone*," she corrected herself, "who touches you, anything that is personal. Your family included. It's not good for you, and it's not good for your country."

"Is that right? And what do you consider I should do about this?" His words were cool, but she wasn't going to stop now.

"Yes, it *is* right. And you should begin with your mother. You're all running scared because she wants to hold on to the power she's always had. But she loves the country. That much is clear from what she's been saying publicly. And so do you. So why not work together? Heal the breach. Make it up. Get her on your side."

"You've been here a couple of weeks and you believe you know things better than my vizier or myself?"

She tilted up her chin defiantly. "Yes, I do. I'm an analyst, I analyze things. That's what I do. *And* I'm an outsider and when you're on the outside you can often see things more clearly than when you're immersed in it."

Malek gritted his teeth but didn't contradict her. "Anything else you care to advise while you're on a roll? Care to tell me I shouldn't agree to an arranged marriage?"

"Yes, actually, I do. You should marry whoever you like.

Marrying a woman from one faction or another will only alienate the others. Marry for love, show yourself to be a real man, with real feelings, and the people will love you. And with love you can do anything."

"Even bring order to a country in chaos," he said facetiously. "Sophie, if only it were that easy."

"It is. Start with making it up with your mother."

"Why are you so concerned about my mother?"

She sucked in a jerky breath and walked over to the door, the anger and emotion and lack of air made her feel as if she were suffocating. "Because you *have* a mother. Cherish her. What I wouldn't give—" She stopped suddenly as her emotions threatened to overwhelm her.

"Sophie?" She heard him walk up behind her.

She turned to him, unable to stop the tears that pooled in her eyes. "What I wouldn't give to have my mother alive for a few more days, a few more months…" She shook her head, unable to continue, and opened the door and walked quickly out, past the curious gaze of his staff, quickening her pace as she heard him call her name once more.

She had to get out of there. She felt like she couldn't breathe in the palace. Everywhere she went there was someone watching her. Everywhere she left, she heard the murmur of voices as they no doubt gossiped about her, conjecturing about what she was doing there and who she was doing it with. She shook her head, trying to rid it of this new paranoia. They were probably talking about the weather. She looked into the unchanging blue of the sun-scorched sky and shook her head. The weather never varied. No, they weren't talking about the weather… They were talking about the woman whose work was putting their noses out of joint, and whose private life their over-active imaginations had no doubt filled with acts that were far from reality. Despite what her traitorous body might wish.

She pushed open the small window which looked out across the city. She felt like Rapunzel stuck in a medieval building with no one to rescue her. She slammed the windows shut. She wasn't medieval. She'd never been someone who was backward in coming forward. She had agency. And she'd use it. She'd leave.

She opened her wardrobe and selected an abaya and hijab.

Half an hour later, with her sunglasses firmly in place, she opened the door quietly and stepped out. She walked past the open office. Several people walked by and nodded respectfully but obviously hadn't the first idea who she was. She continued through the palace and slipped outside.

MALEK PACED the floor of the office, frantic. Staff milled around him, some shouting, others talking on the phone, loudly and urgently.

"Find her, just find her! She can't have evaporated into thin air."

"A guard said someone of Sophie's height just left, wearing an abaya, hijab, and sunglasses. He assumed it was—"

"What color was the abaya?"

"Dark blue."

He looked away to hide his reaction. He remembered a midnight blue abaya being ordered for Sophie.

"Just find her!" He strode out on the terrace and gripped the hot stone. "Sophie, where are you?" he whispered, as his eyes searched the uneven rooflines of the city.

CHAPTER 7

Sophie slipped out of the palace grounds, unseen by the staff. She didn't look right or left, just kept on walking down the wide avenue, buoyed by a mixture of anger and grief. How *could* he dismiss her like that from his life, after what they'd experienced the previous night? *That* hadn't been made up for the crowds; *that* had been genuine. She knew it, she felt it, in every fiber of her being. What was he thinking to be so trusting of his advisers? So distrustful of his own emotions? What the hell had happened to him to make him disbelieve them so utterly?

Her abaya snagged on a piece of stonework that jutted from an old building, making her stop a moment. As she pulled it free she looked around. Where was she? She turned to see the palace looming high above her, and above that, the dun-colored mountains surrounded the city in a semi-circle. To her right lay the busy chaos of a bazaar. She could do without that. But to her left ran a road that curved downhill. She couldn't see where it went, but she knew by the smell. Instinctively she took a deep breath. Intermingled with the scorching dust and the spicy aroma of the food cooking on the open braziers in the market to her right, was the salty smell of the sea.

The street along which she walked had high walls behind which houses stood, once, no doubt, the homes of wealthy merchants, but now they had an air of shabbiness and neglect. For the first time, she noticed that the whitewash was peeling, that tufts of nests poked from the roof-line where birds had made themselves at home. Washing hung from the balconies and signs in Arabic script told of what could be found in the makeshift shops that now lay within. Lofty arched doors opened into courtyards in which women worked and men played dice games and sipped pungent coffee. A small boy kicked a half-inflated ball into the gutter, knocking over an already broken coffee pot at Sophie's feet.

Sophie continued quickly on her way. Somehow the unwanted coffee pot, the beautiful but broken houses, seemed representative of this country. Once great, now needing direction. The only people who appeared busy were the women. She passed a small market in which women— covered from head to foot in black burkas, and carrying small children—selected brightly colored fruit, vegetables, and spices. She moved on, past the bright blue, orange, and yellows of the faded shops, The impressions of this once-great city flicked through her mind as if she were watching a film. She was unable to process them, propelled as she was by anger—anger at Malek's intransigence, anger at the way he still had his mother, but how they hated each other. Only a few more months and then she could be out of here—she could leave this country of false hopes and go wherever she wanted.

It wasn't until she reached the end of the road, when she stopped and stood under a sheltering awning, that it hit her. It wasn't anger she felt, it was grief—grief that he had the mother she no longer had. She'd thought if she ran, and kept on running, she'd outrun the pain of her love, and her loss. But it kept on catching up with her. Malek kept reminding her of what she wanted to forget. And more than that, she'd fallen for him, and she didn't want to fall for anyone.

She shook her head. She needed to move on, to find the fresh air of the sea. She looked around, only to find the way to the sea was blocked by a market, in which there only appeared to be men. On the edge of the market, the men drank, smoked, and talked but seemed totally unhurried. They called to her as she passed, making her walk more quickly.

To the right was a narrow alley which had to emerge at the sea so she went toward it. It was dark in the alley but she could see the sea wall ahead of her, above which white spray splashed into the blue sky. She quickened her step. But then the light darkened and the dark shadows of men, smoking, not talking, came toward her. She remembered what Malek had said about the higher unemployment in recent years giving rise to unrest and violence. She stopped suddenly, menaced by their approaching bulk and quiet, and turned around and retraced her steps to the light of the street. But when she emerged she saw a small group of men separate from the others, who sat under a haze of pungent smoke, and head her way. She took a step back, into the way of other men. She turned in a circle and found she was surrounded by men. There was not another woman in sight.

She pulled her hijab firmly over her face and looked down, remembering what Raisa had advised, and hoping they'd move away. But instead more people seemed to gather, the shouts increased and someone grabbed her arm. She shrieked and jumped, but there was nowhere to go.

"*Assalamu alaykum*" she said, hoping the polite Islamic greeting would hold some sway with them, but there was no polite response, only laughter. "*Assalamu alaykum,*" she repeated.

Then there was a shout, and some police pushed their way through. The sight of police should have been reassuring, but it wasn't. They looked as surly and distrustful as the groups of men who openly stared at her.

One of the policemen barked a question at her in Arabic. He was obviously in charge, but she hadn't a clue what he'd asked.

"I'm sorry..." She shook her head.

There was a murmur amongst the men. The policeman stepped closer and pulled off her sunglasses. "What are you doing here?" he asked, this time in English.

"I'm just walking," she said shrugging, trying to look casual.

"Walking?" The officer half-laughed. "No one walks around here, least of all a Western woman. This souq is for men only." He muttered something in Arabic to his colleagues. They laughed, and she recoiled from their jeering faces.

With one arm of her sunglasses, the officer insolently pushed away Sophie's hair and lifted her chin. He was close now, too close. His thick lips were wet, and she could smell the garlic on his breath.

"You're a long way from home, *habibti.*" There was something in the deepened tone of his voice that penetrated her fear and made her realize the predicament she found herself in.

"I work at the palace. I work for His Royal Highness, the crown prince." She stood herself up to her full height but still had to look up to this man.

He raised his bushy eyebrows in disbelief. "The crown prince?" He spoke a stream of Arabic to his colleagues. They laughed. Then he turned to her. "If you worked for the crown prince, there is no way you would be wandering here alone. Unless"—his eyes narrowed—"he wished you harm."

She shook her head. Her heart pounding with fear. "No, you're wrong." Suddenly she remembered her cell phone. She slipped her hand inside her robe and produced it. "You see, here?" She brandished the phone like a lifeline toward him. "All you have to do is ring and you will get through, and he'll tell you."

He looked at her for the first time with a query in his eyes. He took her phone and twisting it in his hands, he held it up to his colleagues, and they nodded. "You have a top-of-the-line phone. Is this meant to impress me?" She tried to take the phone back, but he pulled his hand away.

"I have the crown prince on speed dial."

He snorted with laughter, and pressed the speed dial as he held it up to the others. "The crown prince on speed dial," he said in English, laughing. Then she heard Malek's voice responding to the call. "Sophie!"

The man's eyes widened dramatically and if Sophie hadn't been so scared she would have laughed.

He brought the phone to his mouth and was about to speak when Sophie again heard Malek shout her name. "Sophie! Where are you?"

Even more alarmed than before, the policeman thrust the phone into her hands.

"Malek," she began. Then she looked up into the policeman's eyes. "Sir! I mean Your Royal High—

"Sophie, are you okay? Where are you?"

She could hear him issuing orders to people in a stream of Arabic while he waited for her reply.

"I'm in the old quarter near the mosque. At some kind of all-male souq."

"Are you alone?"

"Yes. I mean I *am* on my own but the police are here and lots of men are crowding around—"

"My men will be with you shortly. Now, let me speak to the policeman in charge."

She did as he said and handed the phone to the policeman who'd questioned her. He held the phone tentatively to his ear. "Hello?" There was a pause while he listened to a barrage of words from Malek. "Yes, Your Royal Highness." Another pause. "Of course, Your Royal Highness. Immediately. I understand."

He handed the phone to Sophie with a nervous look.

"Sophie." Malek's voice was quieter now, controlled, with the edge of panic gone from his voice. "Do as the captain says. Stay with him there until my men arrive." She twisted around so that the man couldn't see her. "Is it safe?" she whispered.

"Safer than being on your own," said Malek with a distinct chill in his voice. "I want you to keep on the line. I want you to keep talking to me until my men arrive."

She licked her lips, trying to moisten her dry mouth, trying to quiet the chill of fear his words put into her. "Am I truly in danger, Malek?"

"Not anymore."

"I'm sorry," she whispered.

"Just keep talking to me, Sophie."

"What do you want me to say?"

"It doesn't matter. I just want to hear your voice. Tell me anything. Tell me…" He paused. "Tell me about your life in England."

She glanced anxiously at the captain and the small group of three or four policemen he was with, who were being jostled by the crowd as they tried to get closer to her. The calls were coming louder now. They were in Arabic and she didn't understand what the words meant, but she understood the threat inherent in them, and she was scared.

"Speak to me, Sophie." Malek's voice came through the phone once more.

She closed her eyes tight. "I lived in a small village in England. My father died when I was young. My mother brought me up single-handed and she worked two jobs to save the money to send me to university." The shouts grew, as more people emerged to join the gathering. She scrunched her eyes and sucked in a tight breath of hot air that scorched her lungs. "Then my mother got sick. I was sixteen. It wasn't until I was eighteen that we realized what the matter was. She had Alzheimer's. She was only in her fifties. And she had no one but me. I stayed. I didn't go to university. And I looked after my mother. And I worked…" She scrunched her eyes more tightly still as the words and the memories and feelings they evoked became more real to her than her surroundings. She half-sobbed. "God, how I worked! I read, I learned, I looked after my mother. And in time I could afford help for her as she grew worse. And then the end came…"

"Carry on, Sophie," Malek's voice was softer now. "Tell me what happened."

She swallowed. "I had been on the computer, working to a deadline for a client and I had forgotten that the nurse had already left. It must have been seven in the evening. She would have told me she'd left but I didn't hear, I was so focused on what I was doing. I don't know what it was that first made me look up from my work. I don't think there was any sound. There was no change, nothing to alert me that anything was different, but I knew. I felt sick and logged off from the computer. Then I got up and I walked to my mother's room and she had gone. Her heart had just stopped. The nurse hadn't seen it coming. And I hadn't been with her at the end. She died alone." Sophie's sob caught in her throat but she continued. She wanted him to know the full extent of her fears. "And now I'm lost. And I'm so scared. So scared that I'll become like my mother—lost…" Her tears grew to sobs and she couldn't continue. She pressed the phone to her face, trying to cover the tears, trying to hide the sobs, then she heard his voice. She thought it was coming from the phone. But when she felt his hand on her shoulder she realized he was right behind her. She turned and he pulled her into his arms and she sobbed as his men fell in around them, creating a protective shield so nobody could see. He stroked her hair, and calmed her, and then lifted her chin with his finger.

"Sophie, it's okay." He swept her tears away with his thumbs. "It's okay," he said, more quietly now. "Come, let's return to the palace."

He helped her into the open door of a four-wheel drive, which Sophie hadn't noticed arrive. She sat in the cool air-conditioned car and closed her eyes against the white heat, against the crowds and chaos of the city. Malek reached for her hand and held it tight. "I have you. It's okay."

She rolled her head away from him, eyes closed. She should have been reassured by his words, by his soothing touch, but she wasn't. Somehow she felt the opposite. Somehow she felt that nothing would be okay ever again.

DRAINED by the tension in the souq, the memories of her mother, and finally admitting her deeply held fears of losing her own mind, Sophie stared unseeing out of the window, hardly aware that the four-wheel drive had stopped beside an entrance at the rear of the palace, close to the king's private quarters.

"Sophie, we're here." Malek's voice was gentle, as was the squeeze of his hand.

She faced him for the first time since she'd entered the car and saw Malek, the real Malek… the man behind the royal mask.

She smiled. "Thank you. I should have listened to you. I shouldn't have gone. I was—"

She was stopped by the touch of his index finger against her lips as he shook his head. "You don't have to explain. I understand. Believe me," he said with feeling, "I do understand. And it's me who should apologize. I—"

But before he could continue their doors were opened and Malek sighed. "I'll explain later."

"There's no need. I think everything's already been said." She swung her legs and stood, swaying slightly under the blast of heat.

"Sophie, stop."

She stopped.

"Come this way. We need to talk."

They were alone now in the small courtyard. "Surely there's nothing left to talk about?"

"I've been thinking… about what you said."

And she could see that he had. She could see it in his eyes. She followed him over to the door, which he held open for her. Even in this small act there was a change.

Instead of walking down the grand hall toward his suite of offices, Malek turned and walked down a narrower, more domestic looking corridor to a small, comfortable Western-style sitting room which looked out onto the garden they went to on her first night at the palace. He closed the door after her. "No one comes here anymore. My grandmother used to use it. Through the windows she could see what was going on, who was coming and going, and she would summon people to her as required." He chuckled. "Even my father, who, despite ranting against her summons, always went."

He turned around to look at her for the first time since she had entered the palace. He opened his mouth to speak but instead walked over to her, took her hand, and led her to a chair. "Sit down, Sophie. You look dreadful."

She smiled wanly. "Thanks for the compliment." She sat in one of the floral, English-style armchairs and waited for him to say whatever he had to say. It would make no difference. Nothing would. He would shortly be king, and she would never fit into his life. No matter what her feelings for him. Nor his for her, although she didn't kid herself he had any, other than superficial attraction.

"That's your trouble, Sophie. You always make light of the truth. But you're in Sumaira now, and making light of the truth can get you into danger here." He sat on the arm of the sofa.

"I get it, Your Royal Highness. I understand. I didn't before, but I do now."

"How is it when you *should* call me Your Royal Highness you call me Malek, and now when we are getting to know each other you call me Your Royal Highness instead of my name?"

She shrugged. "Contrary, I guess."

He shook his head. "Contrary or infuriating. I haven't decided which yet. Anyway, why did you leave the palace?"

Should she tell him? It was too complicated. Too personal. Best to stick with some version of the truth. "I needed to breathe."

He sighed. "And you couldn't inside the palace?"

"No." If he wanted any more details he'd have to work for them.

"So, you felt trapped. And no doubt our meeting didn't help things. I'm sorry if I upset you. I'm not at my best when handling things like that."

"Personal things, you mean."

"I guess that's partly why I brought you here. It's the place where *I* 'breathe'. The place I used to escape to when my parents argued. They hated each other. I couldn't stand it."

"So you withdrew… to your grandmother."

"Yes, and then, after I left Sumaira, I guess I simply withdrew, period."

Sophie's heart ached for the sensitive boy who first found respite in his grandmother's arms and then, much later, in not feeling anything at all.

He walked over to an antique oak bureau along which old family photos were ranged. He picked one up. "My great-great-grandmother." He showed Sophie the black and white photograph of a tall, lean European woman dressed in flowing clothes, surrounded by Bedouin. "I'd almost forgotten about her. She was one of those eccentric Victorian Englishwomen who explored the Middle East. She came looking for the Spice Route and ended up marrying my great-great-grandfather." He gestured to the very English furniture. "All of this came from her. She was quite a character by all accounts."

Sophie took the photo from Malek, examining this brave woman who hadn't let any limits define her. "And did she ever find the Spice Route?"

"Oh yes. She restored the ancient buildings along the route which runs through Sumaira. It was one of the many legacies she left to this country. Including restoring the ancient castle of Taba, up in the foothills of the mountains. It became our family's second home."

Sophie rose and replaced the photograph. "All I've seen of the country is strife, dissension, and… computers. A bit different to what she saw, I'm guessing."

"Then it's time you saw it. I'll arrange to take you to Taba myself."

"But you're busy."

"I could do with a reminder about this country, about its potential, its history. However I can't guarantee Mohammed will be pleased."

"If we behave, no doubt he'll see it as more photo opportunities."

Malek grinned as he came up to her and brushed her hair from her face. "Trouble is, Sophie, I'm not sure I can behave when I'm with you."

"Then you're going to get into trouble, aren't you?"

"Seems so." He reached out and brought her face around with the soft touch of his finger under her chin. "I never intended any of this, you know." His hands cupped her cheeks and he tilted her face up close to his. "I hired you strictly because of your skills as an analyst. But somehow the personal has gotten in the way." He smoothed her hair from her face. The touch of his fingers played havoc with her heartbeat. "You feel the same way, don't you?"

"That's not a question is it? You're telling me what I feel," she teased.

"I wouldn't dream of it." He narrowed his eyes. "Well, I might dream of it. But there's only one way to know for sure."

She couldn't move under his hot gaze. Before she could do anything, he bridged the small gap between them and kissed her lightly on the lips. But he didn't pull away immediately. He brushed his lips against hers in another brief caress which made everything stand still. It was only when he pulled away that she suddenly gasped for air.

"Why did you do that?" she said, her voice husky. "There are no journalists here, no one to see, nothing to prove."

"Nothing to prove to anyone, except ourselves."

"And what exactly is it you think you have proved?"

He reached over and took her hand, bringing it to his lips briefly before studying the back of it as if some answer lay there. He raised his eyes to her making her stomach flip with desire. "I don't *think*, I *know*. I've proved that somehow we have feelings for each other."

She pulled her hand from his. "Even if we have, what difference would it make? We're from different worlds and have no future together."

"Worlds that have collided." He paused. "We have *now*, Sophie, that's all. Is that enough for you?"

So close to him, his eyes trained on hers, seemingly able to see into the very depth of her, there was no way she could tell him anything other than the truth. She nodded, hesitantly.

"Sophie, I need to be clear. You and me. The next weeks until the coronation. Until I have to choose a wife. Whatever you want. Your companionship, or more. It's your choice."

"My choice? Truth is, I *do* have feelings for you but there's no way I can act on them." She shook her head, needing him to understand. "I like you, Malek, really like you, but I'm not the kind of person who can surrender herself for the moment, knowing that moment will end and I'll have nothing." She shrugged helplessly. "It's just not me."

He grunted with frustration but smiled. "And it's *you* I want. So if it's a working only relationship, so be it. However, it would be remiss of me, as your employer, to keep you trapped within the palace walls. I believe allowing my staff to breathe easily is an essential part of my duties as an employer."

"Mm, breathing is good." Particularly when she was so close to him, and could inhale the masculine warmth of his skin.

"I'll take you to Taba, then, as soon as I can make time."

"But remember this has to be business only. I'm not the kind of woman who can feel something for a while and then turn it off. I've no experience of that kind of thing. I've led a quiet, unsophisticated life."

"I wouldn't say turning your feelings on and off is sophisticated. However, I take your point. If you want business, then I shall make our trip business, just for you. And then…"

She raised her eyebrow, unable to move away from the thrall of his gaze. "And then?"

He drove his fingers through hers and gripped her hand tight. She couldn't have escaped, even if she'd wanted to. And she didn't.

"And then, we'll see…"

CHAPTER 8

The first day after Sophie had escaped into the city had been fine. There had been no time alone with Malek, and everything had been kept to a totally professional level. She'd been relieved.

The second day, Sophie had worked much of it on her own and had had only one meeting which had included Malek. But the meeting was attended by a large number of people and there had been no opportunity to speak directly to him. And it seemed his evenings were no longer his own and she'd received no invitations to join him.

It was late afternoon on the third day when she received the email. It was typical Malek. Short, to the point, and irresistible.

Tomorrow we will go to Taba. Business... of course.

Of course, she answered and closed her laptop.

She felt restless and walked outside, not toward his room, but away through to the older gardens, nodding to the gardeners who'd become familiar to her now. She paused by a wall that was nearly submerged by a colorful climber and bent to smell a flower, caressing its velvety petals before she

stepped onto the path once more, straight into the path of
Malek and one of his men. He stopped immediately, surprise
evident in his face.

"Sophie!"

"Malek!"

The adviser bowed to Malek, murmured some excuse,
and continued walking.

"You will come then, to Taba?"

"Yes."

"There will be a meeting, of course."

"Of course." She felt suddenly breathless.

"What was it you were doing behind the wall?" He smiled.
"Waiting to jump out on me?"

She grinned and held up a flower she'd picked up from
the ground. "Admiring the flowers. They're so exotic, so lush,
so different to the flowers we get in England."

"Beautiful," he murmured, but his eyes weren't on the
flower.

She blushed and looked at the flower, twirling it in her
fingers. "Yes, it is." She drew in a deep breath and looked up
into blue eyes that were still fixed on her. His mouth was a
line of determination, his hands thrust into his trouser pockets. It was all she could do not to reach out and run her
finger along that firm line, relax it in preparation for her
own lips. She sighed raggedly as she tried to contain her
rampant thoughts. What the hell was going on? At the beginning of the week she'd insisted she wanted no other kind of
relationship with Malek than professional. Now, she was
behaving—at least in her mind, and she hoped it would stay
that way—like a sex-deprived woman. Which, she thought
absently, she supposed she was.

"There's been a change of plans," Malek said abruptly. He
walked around her but she stayed still, frozen under his hot

gaze. She felt he could do anything he liked with her at that moment and she wouldn't offer any resistance.

"Yes?" she said faintly.

"The plans for tomorrow are canceled."

She whirled around to face him, not realizing he was so close to her. His eyes were warm. How could she ever have thought them cold? "We're not going?" She felt bitterly disappointed. Had this chance meeting suddenly put him off being with her?

"Oh," he said, as his gaze roved over her hair, her eyes, before they rested on her lips. "We're going. But I can't wait until tomorrow. Go, now, return to your room, and pack your bags. We're leaving tonight."

"But what about the ambassador's dinner?"

"They will have me for months to come but tonight I want to be alone with you."

His words sent a thrill through her body. "I hope you're not expecting too much from me," said Sophie.

"I'm not expecting anything other than your company."

He took one step away and then another. "Go. I'll see you at the rear of the palace in an hour." He walked away, leaving Sophie breathless as she, too, turned and walked quickly to her room. Despite all her rational arguments to herself, and to Malek, she could no more stop herself from rushing headlong into whatever it was Malek had planned than deny the fact she breathed.

MALEK WALKED BRISKLY to the office to inform his staff of the last-minute change of plan. All the while aware of the fact that he'd lied to Sophie. He might not be expecting anything from her, but he was hoping…

An hour and a half later and they were clear of the city. Malek put his foot down on the accelerator and the four-wheel drive shot out into the darkening desert toward the mountains.

"You surprise me," said Sophie.

"My driving? I'm afraid I only do fast and stop."

"No, I'm not surprised at that. I'm surprised that we're alone. No guards in the backseat, steadfastly trying to avoid listening to our conversation. No one to act as my escort, to make sure our respectability is maintained."

"Do you need guards for that?"

"Of course not. But your prime vizier seems to think I do."

"He's not here. And I'll make sure you come to no harm."

"I notice you didn't say anything about protecting my reputation," she said dryly.

Malek's hands gripped the wheel more tightly while his eyes narrowed into the distance. "Indeed. Besides, we aren't alone. Not totally."

"We're not?" Sophie peered behind her seat. "Are they curled up in the trunk?"

He smiled. "I don't think my guards would fit. No, they're in the vehicles behind."

"Where? I can't see them."

"They're not far away. Within radio contact. They'd be here in moments if I called them. But, unless we come under attack—"

"Is that likely?" said Sophie, suddenly anxious.

"Not likely. But it's not unknown. There are still those who don't want to see me on the throne. And those who would force my hand and change my policies. Unless we have to face such a threat, I won't be calling them." He glanced at her. "I want to be alone with you. You know you can trust me. I have my hands on the wheel, and we have a short time in which to talk."

"That's nice." And that was the understatement of the year. She was falling for a man who had everything and knowing he'd set aside his most valuable commodity—time —to focus on her was not only flattering but positively seductive.

"It's only nice if you don't make me talk business."

She tried to cover her smile by looking out the window at the miles and miles of rich, golden emptiness fringed by tall mountains. "I won't. Tell me about where we're going instead."

"We're going to Taba. It's straight ahead. You see the darker smudge in the foothills of the mountains? That's Taba."

Sophie lifted her sunglasses onto her head and peered into the distance. And sure enough, the dark smudge was forming into a castellated wall surrounded by trees which ran up into the mountains behind. "Do the trees follow a river up behind it?"

"Yes. The Spice Route continues up and across a mountain pass into another province of Sumaira—that of my great-great-grandfather's people—which used to be a separate country. Originally Taba was a small settlement where people had to pay a toll if they wanted to pass through. It was here that my English great-great-grandmother ended up."

"I can't wait to see it. I've read a little about it in the guide books."

"I will show you what the guide books know nothing about."

For some reason, Sophie imagined things entirely inappropriate. Things to do with Malek. Personal things. She cleared her throat and chanced a quick glance at him. There was the faintest hint of an upward turn at the corner of his mouth. It seemed she wasn't the only one with wayward thoughts.

She glanced in the wing mirror and saw the two four-wheel drives following at a discreet distance. She was glad they weren't far away. A reminder that they both had to behave. He, for his country's future and she, for her own sanity.

"It'll be quarter of an hour before we reach it. Talk to me, tell me about yourself. Tell me those things that you told me on the phone when you went into the city."

Sophie folded her arms in her lap, suddenly defensive. "I haven't told anyone those things before."

"Really? Why not?"

She shrugged, her gaze fixed on the palace which grew ever larger. "No one to tell really. Besides, it's too personal. I would never have told you if the circumstances had been different."

Malek was silent for a moment. "It must have been difficult for you."

"Not really. She was my mother. I loved her and cared for her until the end. The difficult bit is not having her with me. I always wanted to travel, but now that she's gone, I travel simply because I couldn't bear to be in England without her."

Malek was silent for a moment. "Any other reason why you want to keep traveling?"

"To see the world, I guess. But that's secondary."

"Hm… and you move on before you can form any bonds with people, anything that might hurt you again."

"It's not like that." Sophie frowned as she mulled over what he'd said.

"I'm sorry, simply a guess. Anyway, your mother was a lucky woman to have such a daughter as you. Tell me about her."

Gradually Sophie forgot about Malek's perplexing

suggestion and relaxed as she began describing her mother and her world to Malek.

MALEK TOOK a deep breath of her perfume and let it fill him. The smell of her, her presence got to him in a way that no one had ever done. He'd never felt this way about anyone, not even Veronique. As a judge in the European Union's highest court, the Court of Justice in Brussels, Veronique needed to keep him, ten years her junior, secret, throughout her six-year term of office. And since he'd taken over as crown prince from his brother, there had been no way they had a future. The last time he'd seen Veronique had been in Paris. It had been sad of course, but it had been more anger he'd felt, that he'd had to give her up. He glanced at Sophie. What he felt for her, now, after only a short while, was quite different to what he'd felt for Veronique.

He listened as Sophie talked about her mother and their life together in a small country village in England. He couldn't imagine such a quiet life, such a *real* life. Sophie's words of love and respect filled him with a sense of peace that had been lacking in his life for as long as he could remember. He took his foot off the accelerator a little, allowing the four-wheel drive to slow. Truth was, he didn't want the journey ever to end.

ONCE THROUGH THE large wooden gates, Malek pulled up before an outbuilding. He jumped out and opened the door for her.

"Shouldn't *I* be doing that for *you?*" Sophie asked.

He shook his head. "Definitely not. I may be about to be crowned king, but I hope I haven't forgotten how to treat a lady."

"Wow! I've gone up in the world. I thought I was your employee."

"Not tonight. Tonight, you're my guest." He held out his hand. "This way. I'll show you the wadi first."

They walked through a small grove of tamarisk trees down a small incline. The air changed as they emerged and before them was a small lake, the reflection of moonlight steady on its surface.

Sophie gasped. "This is beautiful."

He took hold of her hand, and it seemed the most natural thing in the world. "Come, let's walk around it."

He looked with satisfaction at the small bay over which a wooden platform had been erected. In the middle was a table and two chairs. The table had dinner for two laid out. Everything was arranged as he'd requested.

Sophie gave a low whistle. "You've thought of everything."

"If tonight is all I have to spend with you, then I want it to be right. Come, stand on the deck—you'll get the best view of the palace from there."

Malek followed Sophie's gaze toward the ancient palace, lit by uplights.

"Malek," she gasped. "This is like something out of a fairy tale."

"Um," he agreed, but he wasn't looking at the palace—he couldn't take his eyes off her. "A fairy tale is exactly what my great-great-grandmother called it in her diary. Of course she didn't see it under electric lights. My father installed these early in his reign."

"Well, it's true. This is the most amazing place I've ever seen."

"There are many more such places hidden in my country. But they remain secret. I believe you are the first European to set eyes on this place in generations."

Sophie's expressive face was full of awe. "Thank you for showing me. I feel honored."

He turned her in his arms and lightly held her hands. He wanted to tell her that it was *she* who made it magical. He wanted to take her in his arms and show her what he felt. Instead, he let her hands fall. "Come, you must be hungry, let's eat."

They walked to the table, Sophie's gaze shifting every which way, his staying focused on her. He pulled out the chair for her and she sat, the silk of her abaya sweeping against his hand. He closed his hand around it briefly, letting it slide through his fingers.

He walked around the other side and poured two glasses of water while Sophie took the lids from the dishes, which were set out along the low table. As he sat opposite, he looked around with satisfaction. His staff had done as he'd instructed, had laid out the dishes and then returned to the palace, leaving the oasis for just the two of them. The palace itself would come later.

As Sophie lifted the lids, he described each of the dishes to her. She sniffed appreciatively at the different aromas. Sophie's delicate profile was lit by the soft apricot lights of the castle and the flickering candles along the table. "So many dishes. Is that usual?"

"It's a sampling of the different specialties of my country. This night is a taste of what my country has to offer."

She picked up the serving spoons and began to serve a selection on two plates. She passed him one. "Allow me, Your Royal Highness," she said with a grin.

He shook his head. "So contrary. Maybe I should insist you always call me that, to get you to call me Malek."

"Worth a try." She took a mouthful of food and closed her eyes and moaned lightly. When she opened her eyes, Malek's glass of water was poised halfway to the table, his eyes still fixed on her.

"It's lovely," she said putting her fork onto her plate, as if suddenly embarrassed. "Can I help you to something else?"

He looked away and replaced his glass with exaggerated care. "You are acting in a very traditional way, Sophie."

She grinned. "Can't have the Crown Prince of Sumaira helping his assistant to food."

He knew she was teasing him but wasn't inclined to respond with humor. "I don't think of you as my assistant anymore. Don't you understand?"

She leaned back on the cushioned chair. "I understand but I also understand when something cannot be. And *this* cannot be. I'm your assistant, but only for a very short while. Then I'll be gone."

"No, you're not my assistant now. Tonight you're my honored guest."

She frowned. "I can't be both."

"You *can* be both."

"I don't agree. Even if I weren't a hired hand, I could only be your honored guest in private. There *is* no future for us."

He sighed and pushed his plate away. He'd somehow lost his appetite for food. "Which of us can say we have a future?" He shrugged. "For me? I could be killed by my enemies tomorrow." He shouldn't have been so warmed by the look of horror on Sophie's face, but he couldn't help it.

"That won't happen, surely?"

He should have reassured her but he didn't want her expression of concern to disappear too quickly. It wasn't much, but it proved she cared in some way for him. "I sincerely hope not. But nobody knows what the future holds. And my father's death was very likely from unnatural causes. The autopsy report was inconclusive. This part of the world is unstable, anything could happen."

He was further rewarded by Sophie leaning forward, her eyes hot and urgent. "You should leave. Return to Europe. Allow your mother or some other relative to rule the country. You said yourself you didn't want to be king. Just leave, just take the next flight out of here so you will be safe in Europe."

"Surely you understand me better than that, by now? I cannot leave here. I've committed to this and will see it through. My people need me to bring stability and prosperity to the country. You've seen for yourself how much work is needed. If my brother were here things might be different. But he's not." Malek couldn't prevent a grim tone from entering his voice. He was annoyed with himself now. He had brought her here to spend time with her, to seduce her if she was willing. Not to argue with her. How had things gone so wrong? But deep down he knew. He knew he couldn't seduce her because she wasn't like any of the other women he'd ever known. "I'm sorry, Sophie. I didn't intend for us to argue. Come, finish eating and I'll show you the castle."

She pressed her lips together and smiled, a brief quick smile that showed the tension and concern was still there. Concern for him, he realized. As he revealed a dish of mouth-watering color and aroma, and she helped herself to some, it suddenly hit him. No one had shown such concern since he'd been a boy and his grandmother had watched out for him. The people he'd surrounded himself with had been too wrapped up in their own lives to show much concern over his. But he could hardly blame them. He'd always been the strong one, the independent one, the one who supported and who didn't need supporting. He still was. So how come this English woman could see beyond the shell he'd built around himself: almost, it felt, see into the heart of him?

By the time they rose from the table, the moon was high in the sky, and they needed no other light to find their way around the lake, to the castle.

As they emerged from the trees, Sophie looked up in wonder. Parts of the castle were in ruins, but other parts were still habitable.

"Come, I will show you around the ruins first. And tell you the stories that my father and his father before him have told."

This time, she took his hand and he curled his fingers around hers. As soon as they entered the ruined buildings, the atmosphere changed. It was cooler amidst the stones partially covered with climbing plants.

"How old is it?" Sophie asked.

"The archaeologists have dated rocks centuries before the Romans came. But the Bedouin tales predate that. It was a village then and a tollgate for travelers on the Incense Route which came before the Spice Route. When the Romans took over it became a place where their soldiers stopped off. It is midway between the Mediterranean and the Arabian Sea. It has always been a strategic place, until now that is. Now it is merely a ruin. But," he added, "it is also a ruin with stories."

"Sounds intriguing. Do tell."

"There are many stories—tales of war, tales of peace, tales of love."

Her gaze took in the moonlight, the sprinkling of stars, before finally settling on the man beside her. "Tell me a tale of love."

"We must walk to the first floor for that. Come." Hand in hand they walked up an ancient staircase which twisted and turned to the first floor where a turret room looked out over the wadi. "My grandfather told me the tale of our ancestor who lived here in this room and was having trouble finding a wife. He had rejected many and had many rejected for him by his own family. And he'd come here out of desperation to escape the pressure. Then one morning he heard singing, and looked at and saw a beautiful woman bathing in the water. He fell in love. And that is how my great-great-great-grandfather married into the Bedouins. There is, of course, more to this tale, but I fear it would be indelicate."

Sophie couldn't tell if it was Malek's voice, deep and seductive as velvet, or the balmy breeze blowing into the ruined windows of the turret, or maybe something else, something needy within her, but something had got to her. She felt it on her skin, flushed and sensitive. She felt it in the tingling of her fingertips, and she felt it inside. Everything moved faster. Her heart raced, her breathing quickened, and she couldn't tear her eyes off Malek.

He stood apart from her, his profile illuminated by the uplights outside the castle wall, but the rest of him was in shadow. His gaze was fixed outside as he retold the old Bedouin tale, his mind far away. For once the hard line of his lips had softened. Suddenly they stopped moving, and Sophie looked up into his eyes, eyes that were now directed to her. The flash of silvered light in the dark depth of his eyes made his gaze unearthly, unreal…and yet even more enticing in its danger.

"Sophie." His voice was huskier than before. "Have you heard a word I've been saying?"

She cleared her throat and went to turn away, but he reached out and caught her arm before she could move.

"Have you?"

"Of course. Well, to begin with anyway and then…"

"And then?"

"My mind wandered a little."

"Ah. And in what direction, may I ask, did your mind wander?"

She shook her head. How could she tell him that she'd

been imagining herself kissing him? She didn't want to go down this track. She couldn't, she told herself fiercely. She shook her head again.

"So you do not wish to tell me." He stepped toward her, letting go of her hand. "Then maybe I will have to guess." He swept his thumbs along her cheekbones and framed her face with his hands. She couldn't move, even though his touch was light. She was mesmerized by his gaze. "Were you imagining *this*?" He dipped his head and pressed his lips to hers. She closed her eyes and surrendered herself to the shock of his kiss—so intimate, so unexpected, like a key turned, unlocking a sensuality she hadn't known she possessed. He drew away too soon.

She kept her eyes closed. She didn't want him to see how much she wanted him. Because there was no way she could act on her feelings. She sighed, opened her eyes and stepped away. She walked purposely toward the door and stopped. He hadn't moved. She didn't turn around. If she saw him, her resolve would fail her. "Malek... whatever I want, whatever I feel, I can't..."

"Of course. I shouldn't want you either, I shouldn't expect... Sophie, there are so many 'I shouldn'ts' but the fact is I want you. And reason has nothing to do with it."

They stood together, not speaking—the only sound was the clattering of palms; the only movement, the flittering and swooping of a bat which cast a shadow between them and the moon.

"I'm sorry..."

She ran down the stairs, trying to stifle the tears that pricked, and the sob that was doing its best to rise in her throat. She hesitated, suddenly realizing she had nowhere to go.

He followed her outside and paused, looked her searchingly in the eyes, but didn't reach out for her. "Time to retire, I think. I'll show you to your room."

They walked in silence, side by side, both lost in their own thoughts and desires, until they reached that part of the castle which had been rescued by Malek's ancestors. When he pushed open the heavy wooden door, Sophie could see at once his English great-great-grandmother's influence. It reminded her of the interior of one of Britain's great monasteries—wooden floors, adobe plastered walls, huge dark wooden beams, and oversized fireplace—except for the traditional Bedouin rugs on the floor and the hunting trophies on the wall.

But Malek didn't stop there. He led her up a sweep of stairs to a large landing from which a number of rooms opened. He indicated one of them. "This is your room." He stepped away as if trying to prevent himself from touching her by putting space between them.

"Goodnight. Call the staff—there are phones in the room —if you need anything."

"Goodnight, Malek. And thank you for everything. It's been a night I'll never forget."

He turned away quickly. She entered the door, closed it, and leaned against it, listening to his retreating footsteps.

She shook her head, trying to rid herself of unwanted feelings, and sternly told herself off. She was doing the right thing, she said over and over as she undressed, slipped on a robe, and pulled back the covers of the bed. *The right thing...* The words drifted into the silence of the night, leaving no trace.

She got out of bed again, and walked across to the window that overlooked the oasis. She could say whatever she liked, but she didn't *feel* as if she were doing the right thing by keeping him at arm's length. She thought over his words about the uncertainty of the future. Of both their futures. Would she ever see him again after her time here was done? Of course not. It wasn't as if they moved in the same circles. No, she only had one opportunity to do what her body so urgently required of her. And it was now. Now or never.

CHAPTER 9

*M*alek switched the shower to full power, needing the stinging jets to convince his body that he wasn't aroused. It didn't work. Suddenly he felt a prickle down his spine and he slammed the shower to off. What was that? Some movement in his bedroom? There were guards placed discreetly around the old palace, and state-of-the-art security triggers would alert them to anyone approaching the oasis. No one could have entered this wing of the palace without him or the guards knowing.

Quietly he stepped out the shower, tied a towel around his waist and opened the door to the bedroom. It was dark. He hadn't bothered putting on a light after he'd returned to the room. But the moon had risen higher now and, despite its slenderness, its light and that of the stars shone through the filmy curtains that should have been still. But they weren't.

The door to the corridor was open to the landing, creating a cross-breeze that blew out the curtains and fluttered around a figure—a figure of a woman. He knew who it was without having to see the details of her face. He could smell the fresh fragrance of her perfume, knew her outline, which had haunted his vision long after he'd left her. It had been that way for weeks now.

"Malek..." Her soft, tentative voice teased his senses.

He paced across to her before she could leave, before she could change her mind.

He placed his hands on her arms, flat at first and then when he'd reassured himself that she was no mirage, he curled his fingers around her slender arms and held her. She was here and he didn't want her to leave.

"You came."

He saw the shadow of the nervous swallow before she nodded. "I—"

He didn't want to hear what she was about to say. He didn't want to risk losing her. And the best way he knew to do that was to show her how unnecessary words were.

He took it slowly at first. He wanted to savor those lips he'd had the hardest time ignoring since he'd first set eyes on her. Their other kisses had been too brief, mere appetizers for what was to come. But not this time. Her lips were as soft and yielding as they looked. He was no stranger to kissing and yet, for the first time, it was as if nothing else existed other than their lips, moving, tasting, gently exploring.

It was Sophie who first broke the spell. Suddenly he felt the pressure of her hands around his back, still damp from the shower, skimming up and over his shoulder blades before smoothing down to his waist. He groaned with plea-sure at the feel of her fingers exploring his body and slipped his tongue into her mouth. He needed to taste her. Needed to taste all of her. She gave a sharp intake of breath before sliding her tongue against his. He felt her slight moan as she pressed her body against his chest. Their hearts pounded, and her hands freed his towel which dropped to the floor.

He pushed his hands inside her robe and what he found

there nearly drove him crazy with lust. She was naked. He closed his eyes as they continued to kiss, and his hands explored the body he'd fantasized about when she'd stood before him, fully clothed, talking of computer systems, or when he'd thought of her as he showered.

Her skin was as soft as silk, and his hands skimmed over it. He had to press closer to her to prove to himself she was real. But her hands felt real enough as they roamed over the contours of his back, closing in on his muscles, sweeping along the sides of his stomach, her thumbs grazing his abdominal muscles, tight with need.

He pushed the robe from her shoulders and kissed the indentation in her collarbone. She moaned, an expression of lust that nearly undid his desire to take things slowly. He hesitated and then continued, exploring her body inch by inch as the robe finally dropped to the floor, alongside his towel. Only then did he pull back and admire the slender curves and fine skin. He traced an invisible pattern of shadow with his finger, watching her nipples pucker as his hand drifted over them. She shivered, and he looked up and caught her gaze, a gaze that was both urgent and scared.

"What is it?"

"It's just that…"

"What? You mustn't worry. I will look after you." He indicated the bedside table drawer where there were contraceptives. "I will do nothing you don't wish me to do." He kissed her. "You don't *beg* me to do," he muttered with a confident smile. But still there was a look of hesitancy and he paused. "If you don't wish to make love, you must tell me now."

"I do. That's why I came. We may have no future, you and I, but we have *now*. I thought about what you said and realized you were right. And I choose *you*. *Now*." She looked away, as if shocked by her own words.

It was all he needed to know. He wanted to take her there

and then but he couldn't. If this was the only time they had together, then he had to make it last, had to savor every moment of it. He had to remember it.

He brought his hand around her neck and tilted her head around to face him. He kissed her hard and pulled away, his forehead against hers. "If now is all we have, then I'll make it a 'now' to remember." He held her gaze fiercely as he put his hands under her bottom and lifted her to him. She slid her legs around his hips and he felt her damp softness against his hard erection. It was all he could do not to tilt his hips and enter her slick folds there and then. But he didn't. Instead, he walked her over to the four-poster bed, and laid her on the ornately embroidered Bedouin spread. He stood and shook his head in wonder.

"You are so beautiful."

She reached over to touch his erection, which grew stronger with each urgent second. He growled and took her hand away. "Not yet." She frowned and he smiled as he knelt before her. "First, I wish to taste you."

She gasped and tried to roll onto her side in a vain attempt to cover herself. He laughed and changed his plan. He lay beside her and kissed her lips, her neck, moving downward, urging her to relax. It did the trick. With each kiss and taste of her tender skin she became less shy, more responsive—her chest rose and fell as her breathing quickened.

When he reached her breasts he moved his nose, his lips, his cheeks over them, enjoying the feel of her tightened bud against his face. It only took a little shift from her, a push of her breast to his mouth to make him realize she was ready. First, he kissed her nipple, then flicked his tongue over it. And then licked it as if it were a rare treat, which it was. She was gasping for breath now, and he realized she was close to coming. Her responsiveness only heightened his lust. Then he took her breast and suckled it hard and she bucked her hips against his, calling out, as the orgasm took over. He continued down, pressing his lips against her stomach and lower.

Sophie was in a state of shock, all modesty forgotten now. Her breathing was erratic, and the blissful release of the orgasm continued to thrill through her while the stimulation of his mouth upon her skin was beginning to stir her body all over again.

He kissed her lower still until he was kneeling before her. He breached her last remaining modesty by gently pushing her legs apart. She watched him but he didn't look at her. His focus was complete, watching the movement of his finger along the lips of her sex which were wet from her orgasm. Despite his own pressing erection, he dipped his head to her sex and licked her, one long lick, taking in the length of her, finishing with a lick and long pull at her clitoris which made her whole body tremble.

"Malek!"

"Um," he moaned as he continued the relentless assault on her body.

"Malek, I…" Whatever she had been going to say was lost as his fingers joined in the exploration of her body, finding their way easily inside her as his seductive tongue swept her body onto a whole different plane.

Gripping handfuls of the priceless woven bedcover, she allowed Malek to take full control, angling her body as he needed to access her sex, holding her limbs which trembled so much. The coiling tensions spun tighter and tighter but suddenly he withdrew and sat up. He reached out to the bedside table before returning to her. This time, their gaze didn't break, as he lifted her legs and positioned his large, hard erection against her sex that was soaked with arousal.

She swallowed, suddenly nervous. But the steadiness of his gaze gave her strength, and she nodded. Only then did she realize he'd been silently asking her permission. It was all it took. And he eased his swollen cock inside her. She lay back and closed her eyes at the bliss of the contact. She angled her hips to take him more fully because she wanted him now, inside her, more than anything in the world.

She hadn't imagined sex to be like this. Neither her mother's old-school romances nor her friends' conversations could have prepared her for the exquisite friction, the way her whole body was alive with feeling, from the tips of her fingers to her scalp and toes that caressed the long length of Malek's legs. And how he filled her—mentally, spiritually, and, not least, physically.

She exclaimed at the balance of pleasure and discomfort and he stopped and looked at her, the expression on his face unreadable. Then she relaxed and shifted. The needs and sensations of her body overpowered the pain. She wanted more. Why had he stopped? She lifted her face to his and with a deep carnal understanding which she hadn't known she possessed till now, she arched up and nuzzled his ear, as her hands cupped his bottom and pulled him inside her deeper. She winced slightly but made sure he didn't see. There was no way she wanted him to stop. He began to withdraw, and she wondered if he wasn't going to leave completely. Did he realize the truth? Did the fact that she was a virgin put him off her? She couldn't let him go. She just couldn't.

"Malek," she breathed, as she flicked her tongue against his ear and nuzzled his neck. "Malek," she half-sobbed, as he made no move, "I need you... further inside me... now." She wriggled against him, urging him on.

His muscles tensed and he exhaled roughly and then he thrust inside her with one long push and she fell against the pillows with a moan of ecstasy.

And then he didn't stop. He moved in and out of her with an uncompromising rhythm, intensifying the sensations within her with each thrust, obliterating any discomfort and focusing her whole being on the movement of his body against and inside her.

Her mind was empty of everything except her connection with this man—physical and emotional—and the exquisite sensations that continued to build, making her cling to his body, demanding everything he had, everything she needed to satisfy her craving for him.

And he gave it, until he too needed to be satisfied. As she cried out, he tensed and his rhythm changed and he came inside her. With a low, satisfied groan, he rolled to his side, pulling her with him. He swept his thumb across her lips and shook his head slightly, frowning.

"Are you okay?"

"Yes, of course." She hesitated, wondering at his sudden quietness. "More than okay. That was wonderful."

"I'm so sorry, Sophie, I had no idea you were a virgin. I'd never have—"

"What?" She searched his eyes for an answer. "Made love to me?"

But he didn't look into her eyes. He stroked her hair and pushed a strand from her face, smoothing its length between his thumb and finger. He focused on the strand of hair as if it were the most important thing in the world. "No, I wouldn't. I have no interest in deflowering virgins." She couldn't place the odd tone in his voice. It was strained and yet there was also a hushed awe in it.

"Well, no. I can believe you don't go searching for virgins. That would be a bit weird."

"Some men do."

"Some men are a bit weird, then," she said smiling, trying to return the atmosphere to a lighter note.

Then he looked into her eyes. "Yes, they are. But I have no interest in using anyone, being responsible for anyone. I'm a loner. Always have been and always will be."

It was her turn to be puzzled. "You'll be king next week."

"Probably the most lonely position of all."

"But you will have a queen by your side. A family."

"I will have a queen, yes. And I will have children, Allah willing, but I won't have a family, not in the sense of the word as you mean it. It is a simple requirement of the position."

Light suddenly dawned on her. "That's why you deleted the requirement that your queen should be a virgin."

"Yes. I don't want that. I don't *need* that."

"But, that's what you've got with me."

He didn't answer.

"You regret it..." she whispered, shocked as she fully understood his words. "You regret what we just did because you don't want any emotional ties, no responsibilities. You don't want me. You just wanted someone to have sex with."

Again he didn't speak. Seconds went by when she could see the warring of thoughts in his head but no resolution. No words. She couldn't wait any longer. Instead, she pushed out of his arms and jumped out of bed. The moon had disappeared and there was only a faint starlight to light her way. She picked up her robe from the floor and pulled it on, keeping her gaze averted from the bed. Tears pricked her eyes, and there was no way she wanted him to see.

She heard him rise and come behind her. He tried to put his arms around her, but she moved away. She took a deep breath, pushed her hair back and faced him. "Don't try to pretend, Malek. Please, do me the courtesy of honesty. Don't say, or do, anything you don't mean. I'm not one of your society women who can understand that. I need truth."

"That's what I'm trying to give you."

"By not saying anything?" She shrugged. "Actually, it doesn't matter. Because the truth is in your eyes."

"It's difficult, Sophie. I'd never imagined you were a virgin. It changes everything."

"How? I've led a sheltered life and I've never wanted to have casual sex. I don't need to do something just to fit in, just for the sake of it. And that makes me unappealing?"

"No, of course not. It shows you have what I already know you have—a strong, determined personality. Someone who lives by her own moral code."

"Then why the whole 'anti-virgin' thing?"

He pressed his lips together and thrust his fingers through his hair. "I've always been with women who are experienced. I made sure of that."

"Because..." she said slowly, as she tried to understand him.

"Because I don't want a needy woman wanting more than I'm prepared to give."

"Give, as in affection, as in love, I suppose you mean. You think you'll sleep with a virgin and she'll be a mewling mess, trying to force you to love her. Well, Malek, it may be hard for your macho arrogance to accept, but not all virgins are needy. Especially this one!"

"I understand your anger." He tried to hold her arms, to still her. "And you've every right to it. I've handled this badly. It's hard to explain."

She crossed her arms. "No, it's not. I understand perfectly. You're scared. You're scared to feel anything for anyone in case it leaves you vulnerable."

"Don't be ridiculous. I'm merely ensuring the women I'm involved with have no expectations."

"Yep, you're scared," she continued as if he hadn't spoken.

"No! It's just that I don't to hurt anyone."

"Well, you've failed miserably."

He tried to reach out to her, but she stepped away. "Sophie, please stay. Let's talk it through."

She took another step away. "You think I want to lie with you and listen to why I'm the opposite of everything you want in a woman? No, I won't stay."

"It's probably for the best," he said dully. "I can't give you the things you want."

"And you would know what I want? Huh? You think I want you to love me, and you can't bear that responsibility." She opened the door and turned to him once more. "Christ, Malek, you're about to be king. You can have everything you desire—including me—and you've taken it, haven't you? And yet you claim the only thing you want is to avoid emotional responsibility. Life doesn't work like that, Malek. And the sooner you understand that, the happier you will be. And the happier your country will be."

With that she walked out the door, slamming it loudly before going across the landing to her room and closing the door firmly behind her. Let Malek think she was angry, let him think she was disappointed with him, let him think what the hell he liked, just so long as he didn't see her cry.

WEARILY, Malek walked to the bed. He looked at the twisted sheets where she'd lain, at where they'd lain together, at where he'd made love to her. How could he have destroyed something so beautiful, before it had only just begun?

He groaned and sat on the edge of the bed with his head in his hands. What the hell had he done?

She'd given him something he'd never asked for in his life

before, something he thought he hadn't wanted, and he had thrown it back at her as it were less than worthless.

He placed his hand on the fine linen sheets which were still warm from her body and lay where she had lain, breathing in the fresh warmth of her fragrance. He'd taken her as if she were nothing, because of his own fears.

He closed his eyes, trying to shut out the images of Sophie that seemed to linger in the room, trying to stop the anger at his own stupid behavior. He'd acted like a fool. He'd spent his whole life avoiding anyone or anything that needed him. And it had been easy when he hadn't needed anything or anyone. But now, for the first time, he felt a connection with someone else that didn't cease when the person had gone. He pressed his hand flat against his stomach. He felt her viscerally, in his gut, in every fiber of his being. It didn't matter if she needed him, because he needed her. But there was nothing he could do about it.

He rolled on his back and watched the shadows of the trees move across the ceiling. Nothing? She was right. He was about to be king. He was lying in the very bed his great-great-grandmother brought from England when she married his ancestor. A marriage of hearts and of cultures. A marriage whose legacy continued to this day. How could such a union be wrong?

CHAPTER 10

*M*alek had been aware of her as soon as she entered the boardroom. He hadn't seen her since the night before—she'd left with a couple of his guards before light had broken—but she couldn't avoid him now.

He hadn't looked her way throughout the meeting, but he could sense her. Briefly, his mind drifted from what his adviser was telling him and he wondered if he'd ever be free of her again. Then he realized with absolute clarity that there was no way he wanted to be free of her. If this was captivity, then he welcomed it. And he knew, in that second, what he had to do.

"Your Royal Highness?"

Malek turned to his adviser. "So what's next on the agenda, Mohammed?"

"The question of your marriage."

"I didn't think it was a question. More of an answer," Malek replied dryly.

"Quite so. Miss Brown has drawn up a list of suitable candidates. Miss Brown"—his adviser nodded to Sophie

—"would like to give us a brief verbal report. Is that satisfactory, Your Royal Highness?"

Sophie cleared her throat and for the first time Malek allowed his gaze to linger on her face. She was pale and tense but from the jut of her jaw on that finely drawn face he could see she was more angry than upset with him. His mouth dried as he watched her open her mouth to speak and he remembered with incredible vividness his lips upon hers, his tongue in that mouth, tasting her, as their bodies joined.

"Your Royal Highness?"

He jerked back his head and attention to his adviser. He nodded. "Of course. Proceed."

He looked at her but she wasn't looking at him. She handed a piece of paper to them both. "Here is the spreadsheet of candidates. I've placed them in order of suitability, with the major points for and against." Malek could detect the huskiness of a sleepless night in her voice.

"Impressive," said the adviser. "And your recommendation? Number one?"

Malek thought only *he* would have noticed the quiver on her lips. It was momentary, but he felt her feelings, had empathy for her like he'd never had for anyone else.

"Yes. Sheikha Talisha of Haraz. Her background is flawless. She's not from this country but is a distant relation of your mother's and, I believe, knew your brother at Oxford."

"So she knows my mother and my brother. That hardly recommends her to me. Anything else?"

"Your country has a long history of strategic alliances, and this would be another. It would strengthen your position."

His vizier smiled warmly, obviously impressed. "You are speaking like a Sumairan, not a woman who has been here only months. You have a good grasp of the country's needs."

"Thank you."

"And the woman herself?" asked Malek, wanting to see Sophie talk of the personal, not the strategic. Wanting to penetrate the façade behind which she was hiding her feelings.

"Equally flawless." Sophie raised her eyes to his for the first time. "You can see from the spreadsheet that her intellect is high. She obtained a first-class degree at Oxford in politics and mixes with high-profile people in diplomatic circles, as well as celebrities."

"But the woman herself?" Malek insisted, steepling his hands before him, focusing more intently on Sophie.

She shrugged. "You can see from the slideshow." She swiveled her laptop around as photo after photo of a beautiful dark-eyed woman filled the screen, some laughing, some serious.

Malek only looked at a few before turning to Sophie. He paused as his gaze settled on her lips—so soft, so powerful. It was all he could do not to stand up and kiss them. "Yes, perfect," he replied, not talking about the woman on the screen—who would no doubt make a perfect queen—but the woman before him who he knew, in every fiber of his being, was perfect for him.

His vizier sat back in his chair, oblivious to the thoughts that dominated Malek's mind. "Good. Pass the details to my assistant. Thank you, Sophie. You may go now."

Malek watched Sophie pack up her laptop and papers and leave the room before he turned to his adviser, his mind made up.

"I don't wish the sheikha to be invited to Sumaira yet."

"You don't want to see this woman?" asked the adviser incredulously. "She's perfect for the job."

Malek winced at the word "job" remembering what Sophie had to say on the subject. "No."

"But she's here already. She's here in an unofficial capacity, and we took the opportunity to extend an invitation for a private meeting this afternoon."

"You did what?"

"You've given no indication you would refuse such a meeting, Your Royal Highness."

Malek sighed. It was true; he hadn't. And he didn't want to create a diplomatic incident. He'd meet the woman but that was it. "So be it. But no more meetings without consulting me. Some additional factors have arisen which I wish to investigate."

The adviser's face darkened but one look from Malek and he bit back whatever he was going to say. "As you wish."

Malek watched him go and immediately picked up the phone. He didn't need advice from his adviser, he needed to know what was legal and what was not. All the rest he'd manage... *they'd* manage, one way or another.

SOPHIE WAS RELIEVED when Malek hadn't tried to contact her again. She'd spent the rest of the day—and night—alone in her room and *that*, she insisted to herself firmly, was *exactly* what she wanted.

Then why, she wondered, as she approached the office early the next morning, was there a flutter of excitement in her stomach at the thought that he might be there? *Get a grip, woman!* she told herself, as she walked into the main office.

But once inside, she paused, looked around, and frowned. Conversations ended abruptly and a mixture of curious and embarrassed glances were thrown her way. Most of the time she'd been here, she'd received polite interest and respect. But now she had the distinct feeling people were talking about her.

"Is everything okay?" she asked the man whose desk was next to hers.

"Yes," he said, without meeting her eye. "And you?" he asked pointedly.

Her frown deepened. "Of course. Why wouldn't it be?"

"I don't know, just thought that your next meeting might be a bit disconcerting for you."

"My next meeting?" For a moment, Sophie wondered if she'd forgotten to add something to her calendar. "You mean the council meeting at two? Why would that be of concern?"

"Not that meeting. Your meeting with—"

Just at that moment the door swung open and Malek's mother stood looking around the small office, eyes blazing. Sophie immediately stood in surprise.

"Your next meeting, with Queen Fairuza," whispered the man beside her as he joined all the others in the room in slipping out the door, leaving them both alone.

"Your Royal Highness," Sophie muttered, wondering what the hell was going on.

"Miss Brown. I was told I'd find you here." The woman's tone was brisk and irritable.

"You've come to see me?"

"Yes, of course. You don't think I'm going to allow Malek to continue on this crazy path, do you? And I know he won't listen to reason, so I've come to you. You can't go ahead with it. It's madness."

"Go ahead with what?"

The woman strode into the room and stood on the far side of Sophie's desk. She leaned forward and gripped the edge of the desk. "Don't take me for a fool. No doubt you had it all planned the moment you set eyes on him, in Paris."

"Your Highness, I really don't know what you're talking about."

"It's no use playing the innocent. My informants are

everywhere, even in the Justice Department. I know all about Malek's inquiries and I'm here to tell you that I forbid you to go ahead with it."

Sophie took a deep breath. "Please, just imagine for one moment that I truly don't know what you're talking about... because I don't. And tell me in plain English what it is you want from me."

"Plain English? I forbid you to marry my son."

Sophie would have laughed out loud if the woman's face wasn't so serious. She was about to contradict her, when she had second thoughts. For one thing, it seemed highly unlikely that this woman would believe her. She had obviously been wrongly advised at the highest level, and nothing Sophie could say would change her mind.

"And why exactly don't you wish me to marry him?"

"I wish him to marry Sheikha Talisha."

"Talisha?" Sophie frowned. It seemed Malek's mother and Malek's advisers were in agreement over this, at least. "Ah... She is a relation on your mother's side, I believe."

"Yes. You may make of that what you will. I don't care to go into details."

I bet you don't, thought Sophie. No doubt the details would be full of political plots and machinations that she had no wish to know. Maybe the queen was hedging her bets—if she failed to resolve her differences with Malek, then at least this woman would give her some degree of influence with him. Sophie could see Malek's future plotted out for the rest of time—a future full of strife and discord and distrust. She was going to be leaving Sumaira soon, and none of this had anything to do with her. But a sudden idea flashed into her head. Maybe, just maybe, she could help him a little.

"Okay. So what's in it for me?" she asked, adopting the mercenary attitude which the other woman so obviously expected.

The woman's eyes narrowed. "How much do you want?"

"I don't want money," Sophie said.

"Of course you do. Name your sum."

"It's not money I want."

"You don't want anything in return for leaving?"

"Oh yes, I do. I'll only agree if you support Malek. After all, he'll be married to your relative, so it's not as if you'll be without influence."

The queen tilted her head to one side. "That's it? You want me to be conciliatory with Malek."

"Yes. Starting immediately."

"And you promise on the life of your mother that you won't marry Malek and that you'll leave as soon as your work here is done?"

The mention of her mother angered Sophie. "I will not promise *anything* on the life of my mother. But you have my agreement and my word."

The queen stepped away from the desk, nodding, obviously trying to decide if Sophie's word was sufficient. "Okay, I suppose that will have to be good enough." She nodded again, this time more decisively. "But make sure you keep your word." She walked toward the door, then stopped and turned around. "You were more reasonable than I'd been led to believe. Goodbye, Miss Brown."

"Goodbye."

The door closed behind the queen and Sophie sighed and sat back in her chair with relief. What the hell had that all been about? Whatever it was about, it seemed that Sophie had been able to make the queen agree to reconcile with Malek without any requirement on her part. She hoped Malek would be receptive. If he would only meet the queen halfway, the country might have a chance at a peaceful future.

Sophie opened up her laptop and clicked on the woman

who was the queen's choice. As it happened, she was also number one on Sophie's list. She glanced at her watch. She had a meeting with Malek and his advisers and she was late.

MALEK NOTICED Sophie slip into the room and take a seat at the rear of the room but kept his gaze fixed on his advisers.

"I can't and I won't," he said decisively.

"Your Highness must deal with your mother's continued influence at court. It undermines you, and your authority."

"You still want me to banish my own mother from Sumaira?"

"Yes, of course."

Malek ground his jaw. It was what all his senior advisers wanted, except his prime vizier who, inexplicably, wasn't present. "I cannot. I *will* not. We aren't living in the Dark Ages here. I will *not* order my mother away from the country of her birth."

"Then what will you do? What action will you take?"

The question hung in the air.

"I have yet to decide. Let's move on with the agenda. We'll talk about this later. What's next?"

"You should talk to her." A soft voice undercut the tension.

Malek and the advisers turned to Sophie as if she'd shouted. It was her duty to speak only when spoken to and to sit quietly at other times. Sophie looked straight at Malek, ignoring the others.

"You should talk to her," she repeated, louder this time.

"You think I haven't spoken with her?"

"Only in anger. Not—" She looked around at the others, as if suddenly remembering her position. "Not in a rational way. Not in surroundings which aren't geared to put her off balance."

The adviser standing in for the prime vizier waved a dismissive hand at her. "What do you know about this? It is none of your concern."

"No, wait," said Malek. "Go on, Sophie. What do you envisage would happen?"

"You said... I believe she grew up as a Bedouin? Why not remind her of her roots, and of your respect for them by setting up a meeting in her place of birth? In Taba. Treat her with respect, remind her that you are her son, remind her that you are sheikh." She paused. "Your Royal Highness," she added.

He could hardly focus on what she was saying. His mind was full of images of their love making—of its beauty and its power—and how he'd thrown it away as if it were nothing.

"You speak well of our culture, Miss Brown," the adviser said, turning to Malek. "If you don't wish to deal with this matter as we have suggested, then that leaves us with little recourse, other than to something like Miss Brown describes."

Malek agreed, forcing himself to focus, suddenly sure. "Sophie, set up the meeting with my mother, as you suggested. Taba will be the place."

Sophie quickly flipped open her laptop and began typing. "Sure. Next week?"

"No. Tomorrow. It has to be tomorrow. Time is running out, and I need my mother's support. Only then will we have the numbers and solidarity to reassure the people, and present a unified front to the world in time for the coronation. Tomorrow, it has to be."

Sophie typed furiously.

"Inform Prime Vizier Mohammed that he is to assist with all the information you'll need to make sure this event is as you first described. Culturally appropriate, conciliatory. You." He indicated one adviser. "Make some calls now. Tell your staff what is required. Set it up." He dragged his gaze from Sophie. "And I want Sophie to be a part of it."

"Certainly, Your Royal Highness," said the adviser. "Now, if we've finished our business here, I believe Sheikha Talisha has just arrived for your first meeting."

Malek frowned. He'd agreed to the meeting to buy time, but he wasn't looking forward to it.

"With your marriage to the sheikha," the adviser continued smoothly, "and with diplomacy such as Miss Brown describes, it would be a fresh start for the country."

Malek glanced at Sophie and rose. The woman who he couldn't get out of his mind had given him something that no one else had—a future for his country. But, as far as she was concerned, a future without her. It proved she wasn't right about everything.

~

SOPHIE CLOSED the computer and checked the time. He should have finished his meeting with Sheikha Talisha by now.

Despite burying herself in work all afternoon, she couldn't help wondering how the meeting was going. She'd thought of nothing else, imagining how he'd react to that luscious beauty.

She leaned against the side of the window and folded her arms protectively around herself. Despite the warmth of the evening, a shiver tracked along her spine.

How else could it have gone? The woman was beautiful, intelligent, and apparently charming. Ditto Malek. She closed her eyes. She'd been crazy to think she could carry this out without getting involved. Every inch of her body was involved.

Just at that moment there was a sharp rap at her door.

Sophie frowned. Raisa wasn't due for another hour to help get her ready for dinner.

She walked over to the door and opened it. Malek stood at the door, an exasperated yet amused look on his face.

"Malek!" She stepped back into her room in surprise.

"You knew, didn't you?"

"Knew? What?"

"May I come in?"

"You will be king. I guess you can always command me anyway."

"Okay, I command you. Allow me entrance!" He smiled but she didn't smile back.

She opened the door. "Of course, Your Royal Highness."

"*Malek.* I'm Malek to you."

She stayed by the door as he prowled into the room, glanced at her office, at the gown lying on the bed. He walked to the table and picked up some papers, riffled through them and came to the spreadsheet. "You certainly gave me what I wanted with the sheikha."

"Of course."

"Intelligent."

"And she is, is she not?"

He paused, drew a breath as if to say something, glanced at Sophie, and then slapped the papers with his other hand, dismissively. "Yes. She spoke well."

"And that is what you wanted. A good communicator. Didn't you enjoy conversing with her?"

"No."

"What did you talk about?"

"I don't know. She talked and I couldn't concentrate. She just wasn't…" He shook his head. "And for another thing… her looks."

Sophie was beginning to get irritated. "What's wrong with them?" She picked up her photo from the open file.

"You can't deny she's absolutely beautiful. Those eyes, they're—"

"Cold is what they are."

Sophie raised an eyebrow and looked at the photo. She supposed the sheikha did look a bit off-putting, a little cold. But then she was the sheikha, a powerful figure in her own country. And with the scope to become an even more powerful figure when she married Malek. She looked up at Malek. "You didn't state you wanted 'warm,' Your Royal Highness." She looked at the photo again. "Although her lips look pretty warm to me." Too warm, she thought, reluctantly admiring the full, pouting lips.

"I don't know. I didn't notice. I was too busy trying to avoid listening to her speak." He turned an accusatory glance at Sophie. "Have you heard her voice?"

Sophie shrugged, suddenly remembering the shrill tones she'd heard on one particular video. "Maybe."

"Maybe? You haven't then. Because once heard never forgotten. The sound alone would drive me crazy."

"Come on, it wasn't that bad. She sounded pretty normal to me."

"No, she didn't. Her voice wasn't agreeable enough by half."

"I'm sorry, you didn't specify the timbre of her voice in your long list of requirements."

"I didn't think I had to." He sighed, as if suddenly realizing how absurd his arguments were. "You were one hundred percent correct about one thing."

"I'm glad my research proved useful for something. What was it?"

"She'd make an excellent queen."

She folded her arms, perversely not liking the fact that he agreed with her. "So what's the problem?"

He raked his hands through his short hair, moving it not an inch. "I can't marry her."

"But I thought you just said—"

"I know what I said. And I'm still saying, I can't marry her."

It was Sophie's turn to feel angry. After the intimacy of their night at Taba, he thought he could just turn up here and find fault with Sophie's work on finding him a wife. She hadn't imagined he could be so unfeeling. She walked up to him and took the file from his hand and held it up to him. "You said she was perfect. I've done what you wanted me to do and I've found the perfect wife for you."

"No, you haven't."

He took the file from her, closed it, and dropped it on the desk.

"Malek! You're being unreasonable."

"No, I'm not."

"Yes, you are. *She*"—she stabbed her finger at the sheikha's closed file—"is the perfect wife for you."

He stepped closer to her and captured her finger in his hand and held it tight. She tried to pull away, but he was too strong. "No, you didn't find me the perfect wife. You found my *kingdom* the perfect *queen*. They are *not* the same thing."

"What the hell do you mean?" She'd forgotten everything now. Forgotten he was about to be crowned king, forgotten she was a lowly servant. All she could see was the man who'd so tenderly made love to her just a few nights before, the man she wanted more than anything else, standing before her, angry with her for not finding him the perfect wife.

"I *mean*, you haven't done your job properly."

"I've done my job perfectly. You should marry her."

"I can't."

"Why not?"

"Because..." He suddenly dropped her hand and stepped

away from her. He opened his mouth to speak but instead walked away. He paused, with his back to her, his hand on the door handle.

"Tell me why, Malek. I need to know."

He turned to her with a look of absolute defeat. "You know why."

She shook her head, as she tried to suppress the answer her heart gave her. She managed it easily as reality and logic overtook her thought processes. "No, I don't. I have no idea."

He didn't speak, which made her more nervous. What the hell was going on?

"It can't only be the voice, the cold eyes…"

"No." He looked down and then up with a different expression in his eyes. "It's not. Have you no idea? Really, after Taba?"

She shook her head. "Taba? You were angry with me."

He reacted as if she'd struck him. He reached out, but she stepped back.

"I'm sorry, Sophie. I'm so sorry for how I reacted. It was a shock, that's all. Something I've avoided all my life and suddenly it's there, in front of me, and I…" he shrugged helplessly. "I reacted badly."

"That's the understatement of the year."

"Forgive me, Sophie." She tried to move away but he caught her hand and held it tightly.

"No! You were a bastard."

"I don't think you're allowed to call your crown prince a bastard."

"You said you're Malek, just Malek. You seem to change your mind to suit yourself. Am I with the soon-to-be-king or with the man?"

"You're with the man who regrets his stupidity. It's haunting me. *You're* haunting me. I can't think of anything else but you." He paused. "Tell me you forgive me."

She shouldn't. He'd hurt her deeply but she could feel herself relenting. The way his fingers moved over her closed fist, trying to massage away her defenses, mirrored the way his eyes tried to bring her around. And it was working.

"I... shouldn't."

"But you will?" he asked gently. "I know it's a lot to ask, but I truly am sorry. I wouldn't hurt you for the world, believe me."

She sighed. "Seems I have no choice. Seems I can't hold anything against you."

He smiled, one of his rare and totally engaging smiles. Sophie reckoned if he'd done that as soon as he'd entered the room she'd have forgiven him immediately. Not that she'd tell him that.

He closed his eyes and exhaled with relief. She hadn't realized until that moment how much he was waiting to hear her say the words of forgiveness. "Good, good."

"Although I can't see why you're so worried."

"Because I have something else to ask you."

She shook her head. "There is no better match for you than Sheikha Talisha. You'll get used to her voice."

"No, no I won't. There's only one voice I want to hear on waking, during the day, and going to bed. Only one voice. Don't you understand, Sophie? That's yours."

Sophie opened her eyes wide. "What?"

"Sophie." He smiled, more uncertain now. "I've looked into it from the legal angle. There will be obstacles but none that can't be overcome."

She shook her head in disbelief. "What are you saying, Malek?"

"I'm asking you to marry me. I had no idea I could feel this way for someone, no idea how consuming it would be. I need you, Sophie. Please, marry me."

Sophie felt as if she were in a dream. His words were

unreal, unbelievable. But... there were no words of love, she had no idea if what he felt would last. She hadn't even any idea of what *she* felt for *him*. She hadn't dared examine the deep passion she felt for him for fear of what she'd find. Because where there was love, there was pain.

And then the other reasons why this marriage could never happen came crashing down on her: Malek would be king and his country depended on him making a good marriage. And lastly she remembered her promise to his mother.

Her mouth dried. She tried to speak, but no words emerged.

"Sophie?" He rose to his feet and pulled her toward him. "Sophie, what's wrong?" He pulled her against him and held her in his arms and she wanted to stay there forever. But forever lasted only moments, until he pulled away and tilted her tear-stained face to his. "Tell me, what's wrong," he insisted.

"I can't marry you," she whispered. "I'm sorry, Malek, but I can't."

"Why? I thought you had feelings for me. Don't you?"

She shook her head, remembering her promise to his mother not to breathe a word of the arrangement.

He stepped away from her. "That's it, isn't it? You simply don't feel enough for me. I'd thought you did, but you don't, do you?"

Again she shook her head as words refused to form from the jumble of thoughts that whirled in her brain. She turned away, unable to look him in the eyes and witness the suffering there. By the time she wiped her eyes with the heel of her hand, he'd gone.

CHAPTER 11

*M*alek looked around the ruins. Sophie had done a spectacular job in such a short space of time. And it had all gone to plan. He glanced at his mother who was happily regaling a cousin with news of the latest Paris fashions.

At first, the queen had refused to attend. It had taken additional words from his prime vizier to persuade her. Malek didn't know what the particular words were, but whatever his vizier had said, had worked. After an initial reticence, she'd soon relaxed and participated with a good will which Malek hadn't seen in her for years.

And it was all down to Sophie. Where was she? He glanced around the ruins which Sophie had re-created as the oasis it would have been during important feasts, complete with traditional Bedouin colors and fabrics.

The soft desert evening breeze made the fine silks shimmer and shift around the vast table. The table itself was laden with traditional food—heaped greens, oranges, reds—jewel-like decorations in themselves. Vessels of traditional beaten copper reflected the light of torches which were thrust into the ancient stone sconces of the Roman pillars.

There were twenty guests, ranging from the very young to the very old. If they had been surprised at the sudden invitation, they didn't show it and were simply happy to see each other. Sophie had somehow managed to track down key family members from all across the country. It had been a long time since they'd been together and any strangeness at this sudden summons had been easily overcome by their obvious pleasure at seeing each other again.

And it was a pleasure which only deepened as past wrongs were forgotten, if not forgiven, and animosity was put to one side in favor of family unity. Now, as the feast was drawing to a close, people sat on the traditional cushions and listened to the musician who sat cross-legged to one side, singing and playing a *rababa*, his voice full of emotion as he sang of heroes of the past.

But Malek wasn't concerned with the past as he looked around surreptitiously, trying to locate Sophie. He was concerned with the future. He turned at a touch to his arm.

"It's been a wonderful evening, Malek." His mother inclined her head to his. "A few days ago I couldn't have imagined you'd have come up with something like this. I don't think many things could have touched me as this has. You've done well to bring the family together."

"Not all the family, unfortunately," said Malek.

"Jaish?" asked his mother.

"Yes, he should be here."

"If he were here, you wouldn't be crowned king."

"No," Malek sighed.

Queen Fairuza frowned as she studied Malek. "Malek, you're my child and yet I've never understood you... least of all now."

He gave her a sideways glance. "No, I don't suppose you do."

"Do you truly not want to be king?"

"Has that thought only just occurred to you? Can't you imagine any scenario where someone might not want absolute power?"

"No, I can't. Although you were always a strange boy growing up."

"Is that why you gave all your attention to Jaish?" Malek was surprised to hear the bitterness which edged his words. He'd thought he'd buried that long ago.

The queen took a sip of water thoughtfully. "It was easy to love him. He was open and engaging. You were always reserved, spending time with your beloved grandmother. You know, I was always a little jealous of your relationship with her."

Malek shook his head. "You shouldn't have been. It was *your* love I craved."

The queen put her hand on his arm. "Ah, my son. Such a complicated web of love, need, and ambition. I'm sorry for it all. But maybe, after tonight, we can start afresh."

He raised his glass to his mother's. "New beginnings."

They clinked glasses. "New beginnings," she repeated, taking a sip of water. Then her eyes narrowed, as she looked over Malek's shoulder. "Is that…"

He followed her gaze, just in time to catch a glimpse of Sophie's face from behind a curtain. "That's Sophie Brown."

"Hm." His mother frowned. "She's certainly pretty. I can see why you wanted to marry her."

Malek turned his gaze slowly to his mother. "How on earth did you know that?"

The queen waved her hand. "I know many things, Malek. I've lived in Sumaira all my life and know more people than you can imagine."

Malek studied his mother's face and frowned. "You used the past tense. You said 'You *wanted* to marry her.' Why would you think I don't want to anymore? Why would you think that we won't be marrying?"

The queen smiled at him, said nothing, and beckoned the waiter to fill her glass.

She knew something. His mother knew what only he and Sophie knew—that Sophie had refused him. He didn't know how she knew this, but he'd find out.

He rose. "Sophie!" he called, as he watched her try to retreat into the shadows. "Sophie!"

SOPHIE PEEPED from behind the tent where the food had been prepared. She was satisfied and relieved with how it had gone. It had been a gamble, but the care she'd taken over setting up the venue and invitations which had been personally made by Malek's prime vizier—who, it turned out, was a relation and wielded more power than she'd known—had paid off. Everyone looked happy; even the queen and Malek were chatting as if they'd never fallen out so spectacularly.

Malek… She swallowed hard, trying to hold in the tears at the thought of not being able to be with him. But she couldn't do it to him, or to his country, or to herself. If it felt like this now, imagine the pain she'd feel if he left her when someone he truly loved came along. No, she'd leave as soon as she could. She wouldn't stay for the coronation, no matter what Malek said.

She backed away and released the curtain which she hid behind, but a gust of wind suddenly rose from nowhere and it billowed out, revealing Sophie to everyone. The queen looked up and saw her. Her face darkened.

Sophie froze as she watched Queen Fairuza and Malek exchange words. Then Malek looked at her and she started to leave. He called out to her and she stopped in her tracks, not wanting to do his bidding, but unable to refuse.

"Sophie!" he called out again. She inhaled, pushed aside the curtain, and walked toward him.

"Sophie, please come and join us," said Malek.

"Really?" said Queen Fairuza coldly. "Do you think that's wise, Malek?"

The queen gathered her flowing robes as if to rise from the table but Malek put a firm hand on her shoulder and the queen looked at him, astonished.

Sophie could have kicked herself. Everything had been going so well until now. Queen Fairuza had appeared to have softened, and she and Malek were talking without biting each other's heads off.

Sophie looked behind her as if for escape. Instead, her retreat was blocked by children playing. She turned to Malek and his mother, unsure what to do. She bobbed a polite curtsey. "Your Majesties."

The queen nodded, tight-lipped. "What's this about, Malek?"

"I thought you'd be interested in the fact that Sophie set this whole thing up, Mother. In fact, this was all her idea."

"Really?" The woman narrowed her eyes. "You, and all your advisers, couldn't have thought of this yourselves?"

Malek didn't look perturbed by the insult. "Apparently not. It took Sophie to show me the importance of family. Sophie, please take a seat."

"Well, I…" She looked around, desperate for an excuse not to join them. It could undo all her hard work.

"No excuses." Malek signaled for the waiter to pour her a drink. "Allow me to introduce you to my mother properly. The last time you met was in Paris, was it not?" He glanced from one to the other.

Sophie and the queen exchanged a cool, complicit glance.

It seemed neither would say anything about their second meeting.

He shrugged. "And the atmosphere then was heated, to say the least." He turned to his mother. "Mother, this is Sophie Brown."

"Sophie," the queen acknowledged. She glanced from Malek to Sophie and obviously decided it was in her best interests to at least appear friendly. "I would never have guessed that someone outside our culture could have organized tonight's feast."

Sophie gave a brief nervous smile. "I didn't do it on my own. Prime Vizier Mohammed helped, as did many others. I just brought it all together."

"Don't be so modest, Sophie. You should claim your success."

Sophie looked nervously at Queen Fairuza. "I don't want to claim anything that's not mine."

"As is right." The queen cleared her throat. "I believe you're here for only a short while, Sophie. When do you leave?"

Sophie determinedly avoided looking at Malek. "Tomorrow," she said quietly.

"What?" asked Malek.

She turned slowly to him. "Tomorrow," she repeated.

He frowned. "I haven't given permission for you to leave yet."

"No, but given the circumstances I thought it might be better if I leave sooner rather than later."

"Sophie is quite right, Malek," said the queen. "Her work here is obviously done. And you need to focus on your future," she said pointedly.

"You're not leaving yet, Sophie. I forbid it."

She raised her eyebrows. "You forbid it?"

"I *want* you to stay."

"I can't," Sophie said, willing him to understand, to accept the fact that their future was not together.

"Let her go, Malek," said his mother quietly.

"I can't do that, Mother."

Sophie had to look away. His feelings for her were obvious—there for everyone, including his mother, to see.

"Oh," said Queen Fairuza shortly. "Well, I can see what Malek sees in you. But you both realize it can go no further. Affection, love, whatever you wish to call it, is irrelevant in your future relationship, Malek. You do know that, don't you?"

Malek didn't take his eyes off Sophie, but his words were for his mother. "My great-great-grandfather married a woman like Sophie. An English woman."

A quiet descended on the table and the Prime Vizier Mohammed rose and stood beside Malek.

"He's right. It's hard to imagine, but in days gone by our courts were not as insular as they are now." He looked at Sophie. "Our people have always been open to good people, no matter their background." He acknowledged Sophie. "And when Malek's great-great-grandmother arrived looking for adventure she found it in the form of his great-great-grandfather who immediately fell in love with her."

Malek exchanged glances with Sophie as the vizier fell silent, his gaze on the queen.

"Nothing is greater than love, Fairuza. Love for family, love for people."

Queen Fairuza's expression crumpled a little under Mohammed's scrutiny. Mohammed placed a hand on her arm, and she closed her eyes and looked away. But her hand crept over his as she nodded.

Sophie glanced at Malek. It was clear from his expression that whatever had just passed between Mohammed and the queen had been news to him. It seemed that Malek's father's best friend and chief adviser loved the queen and no one had known… except the queen.

"You're right, as always, my friend," the queen said. "I should have listened to you years ago, but I'll listen now."

He indicated his approval. "Good. Tomorrow we will meet, Fairuza. Tomorrow we will begin again." He bowed and left.

Malek, too, rose to say goodnight to his family, who had already begun to drift away to the scattering of tents, which had been erected to accommodate the extra guests.

With only Queen Fairuza remaining, Sophie went to leave. This time it was the queen who reached out to her. She laid a hand on her arm.

"Stay, Sophie. Please stay."

Sophie took the cushioned seat next to the queen and they sat in silence, watching Malek swing his young cousin up in his arms in a playful gesture before handing him to his mother.

"My son has always loved children but never allowed himself a family. But now, I see a change in him."

"Truly?"

"You doubt it? I thought you were more perceptive than that."

Sophie watched Malek playing and realized his mother was right. While Sophie had been working hard to distance herself from close relationships, Malek had done the opposite. As the doting cousin, the attentive son, he was nothing like the man she'd first met.

Queen Fairuza narrowed her eyes on Sophie. "I know you're clever. The way you organized tonight. Genius. Elegant in its simplicity and effectiveness. And yes, in case you're wondering, I know when I'm being manipulated."

"But—" Sophie was suddenly terribly worried that it had all gone wrong.

The queen smiled and shook her head, her eyes kind for once. "But that doesn't mean I haven't wanted to. Contrary to popular belief"—she cast a wry glance at Malek—"this was exactly the sort of opportunity I desired." She paused, obviously seeing the incomprehension and disbelief on Sophie's face. "Malek isn't the easiest person to talk to, particularly as he surrounds himself with all those ministers." The queen rolled her eyes briefly before settling intently once more on Sophie. "Things have been bad between us for some time. I'm closer to his brother. Maybe it was that which drove him away." She shrugged. "But I'm still Malek's mother with a mother's feelings, whatever he may think. You are not a mother, I think, and yet you somehow understand. How is that?"

"I am, I mean I *was* close to my mother. I cared for her when she was sick for many years. When you work from home, and your world is narrowed to a few people, I think maybe you get to study them to understand them better." She got her emotions under control. "I don't know. Or perhaps it's simply because I'm an outsider. I could see the common ground which could bring you together."

The queen nodded slowly. "Malek always did have excellent taste. Even in that judge he secretly courted for so many years, the one he thought no one knew about. My son and I have been strangers too long." She reached over and took her hand. "I have a lot to thank you for."

Sophie lay in the bed of the tent she'd been allocated, listening to the murmur of voices of people still seated outside, who were unwilling to call it a night, when she heard footsteps approaching.

"Sophie?"

Sophie rose and lifted the flap of the tent. "Malek," she

breathed. Silver starlight outlined his silhouette.

"May I come in?"

She stepped aside in answer.

He walked in and looked around. "Your tent is small."

"It's fine for me."

"No, it's not. Nowhere near fine enough for you."

There was something in the controlled urgency of his voice that made Sophie's heartbeat quicken. "Why are you here, Malek?"

"I came to thank you."

"You've nothing to thank me for."

"I've everything to thank you for. The evening was an unprecedented success. My mother hasn't left as we'd imagined she'd do but has decided to spend the night here so the meetings with our people may continue tomorrow. It's cemented our relations like nothing else could have done."

"Thank goodness."

He took her hands in his. "Sophie, have you reconsidered?"

She pressed her finger against his lips. "Don't, Malek, please. Don't speak of it. Not now."

He kissed her finger. "I'll be king in a few days. All-powerful in this country. I can snap my fingers and have whatever I want. Anything, apparently, except you. Why can't I have you?" His gentle, questioning tone nearly undid her.

She shook her head. She wasn't going to tell him. She wanted no arguments—only him, in her bed. "You remember when we made love last time? Same deal applies. For now, you can. But just for now."

"But Sophie, I have no protection for us here."

It was the last thing on her mind. It was impulsive, it was reckless, but all she wanted was him inside her one more time. Completely.

"I don't care, Malek. I want you now."

He closed his eyes slowly and reached out blindly for her and pulled her against him. He kissed her head and rubbed his cheek against her, holding her tight. Then she felt a shudder travel through his body, and he lifted her face and kissed her, not gently, but with a raw passion that burned away any of her lingering doubts.

His hands pushed up under her shirt, sweeping over her bare skin, before deftly unhooking her bra. With her breasts free, he moved from her mouth and kissed her throat, pulling open her shirt as he did so, the buttons ripping away from the material in his haste. He moved lower, his lips seeking out her breasts which he held in his hands, offering them up to his mouth to taste. And he did, one after the other.

She dropped her head back allowing him greater access and moaned as he suckled the tight nub of her nipples. "Oh, Malek," she whispered, as his hands undid her pants. He pulled them off her and tossed them to one side, leaving her naked in the flickering light of the candles.

He shook his head as he looked at her. "You are beautiful, Sophie. So beautiful. And to think I was ungrateful for the gift you gave of yourself."

She trembled under his gaze, which practically devoured her. She reached out to him. "Malek," she pleaded, "take off your clothes."

He raised his eyes with a seductive smile. "With pleasure."

It was her turn to watch as he tugged free his buttons and threw aside his shirt. But he was going too slowly for her and she undid his buckle and slid down his zipper. He pushed his trousers away and stepped out of them.

She jumped into his arms and kissed him. He put his hands under her bottom and she slipped her legs around his hips, his erection pressing against her wet folds. She gasped as it made contact with her clitoris. He shifted her in his arms and slid into her.

She wriggled against him as they continued to kiss. He thrust into her and her body easily accepted him this time—more than accepted, *needed* him. She met each thrust with a gasp and moved in time with his rhythm. She pulled away from the kiss and sunk her mouth onto his shoulder to try to stifle her cries. And he gripped her more tightly still as he thrust inside her repeatedly. With the final thrust he cried out his release, and she kissed him to take his cry into her mouth.

He slowly relaxed his grip on her and walked with her in his arms over to her bed. They lay on their sides facing each other, his arms still around her.

"Sophie," he whispered, and the sound was like the desert wind drifting through the tall trees in the oasis. "I can't let you go." She opened her lips to reply, but he kissed her and then pulled away, his finger tracing her lips. "Don't say anything because I don't want to hear it."

"I'm to say nothing at all?" She smiled.

"No, nothing."

"So I will have to express what I want to say with my body?"

He nodded.

Tentatively she moved her hands from his shoulders, along his arms, muscled and toned, to his hands and then to his hips. The only men she'd seen naked before had been in films. Never before had she touched a man. She moved her fingers tentatively to his growing erection, stroking gently down his length which grew longer under her touch. She licked her fingertip and rubbed the end of his cock. It was smooth and a pearly drop formed under her finger. She smoothed it over and drew her finger to her mouth and licked it. It tasted of them both.

Malek groaned, rolled her onto her back, and took both her hands in his and pushed them high above her head, pinning her hips with his.

"I have you helpless, now." She opened her mouth to speak, but he silenced her with his mouth. "Remember what I said... no talking." Then he released her and moved along her body, first kissing her breasts and then moving further down, he kissed her sex. She moaned. "No talking... only sounds of pleasure are to escape your lips."

She swallowed as he kissed her again. But this time he didn't stop at kissing. And she bucked against the bed, her hands on his head but now, instead of trying to bring him back to her, she held his head in place, and moved against him with an abandon she didn't know she possessed.

The moans and soft sighs he wanted to hear came more quickly now, and louder, as he continued to pleasure her. She gasped and called out his name as she exploded with an orgasm that left her breathless.

Only then, with a final lick, did he push himself up and look at her. "You taste as good as you look, my love."

She felt totally wanton now; all shyness had fallen away under the barrage of orgasms. She drew her legs together until they'd trapped his erection between her thighs. He drew a sharp intake of breath.

"Haven't you had enough yet, my insatiable Sophie?"

She shook her head, keeping to the game of not speaking. Instead, she opened her eyes into an innocent gaze, opened her legs into a totally non-innocent position and rolled over until she was on top of him.

She rose to her knees, took his cock between both her hands and held it against her, rubbing him back and forth along her soaking sex, watching him from under lowered lashes. A muscle ticked in his jawline, as he gripped her hips and pushed her onto him.

It felt different to before, the angle she guessed. She shifted around and gasped at the rub of her clitoris against his tight belly. Slowly she rose, feeling the moist drag of him inside her. God, she never wanted this to end. She leaned over him, placing her hands on his shoulders, shoulders so wide and strong, so capable of anything, and yet wanting only her. With her breasts grazing his chest she continued to move up and down, over him, watching the expression on his face intently.

She felt immensely powerful, as she watched him react to her movements, changing her rhythm or her position to see what effect it had on him; dipping her head and trailing her tongue against his lips, but lifting away just before he could kiss her properly. The teasing worked. She could see it in his eyes. It made him thrust deeply inside her.

She dipped again and kissed him this time, allowing the hardened tips of her nipples to rub against his rough chest hairs. She didn't know who she was giving the most pleasure to—Malek or herself. Finally, she could take no more, and they both exploded in a simultaneous orgasm. She fell against him, totally spent.

Gently, he folded her in his arms, and they lay entangled, as their breathing returned to normal. She closed her eyes and drifted away. The last thing she remembered was his soft endearments spoken in a language she didn't understand, but whose meaning she understood completely.

Sophie awoke with a start to find light had broken, people were up and about, and Malek had gone. She checked her phone for the time. She was late but then her duties were over. She wasn't required for anything. The thought was sobering.

She wasn't required for anything anymore. She'd done

her duty—she'd written a detailed report on the palace's IT systems, interviewed and trained her replacement, somehow managed to set the royal family back on their way to healing and, lastly—the accomplishment which made her feel sick to her stomach—she'd found her lover a wife.

She swung her feet onto the woven rug and swept her hair out of her face. So it was time for her to go. There was no need for her to stay for the coronation, no matter what Malek said. No matter what he wanted. She'd promised his mother they wouldn't marry, and the country's peace and prosperity depended on that promise.

No, she'd be gone before he knew. She'd hitch a lift with the caterers returning to the city. Malek wouldn't know. He'd be too tied up with his visitors.

WITHIN HALF AN HOUR Sophie was in the caterer's van. If they thought it odd, they weren't saying, which was fine by Sophie.

She leaned her head on the headrest and looked across the plains. How could she have thought these plains were unending and monotonous when she'd first arrived? Now she could see their subtleties: the different patterns the wind had played with the sand, the different images the cloak of light created at different times of day, the dark, charcoal smudges that were the first indication of life, the misleading mirages of flickering water where there was none.

It should still feel strange—after all, she hadn't been here long. But it was Malek's home. She closed her eyes and remembered his arms around her, his body inside her, and knew that whether she liked it or not, wherever he was, would be her home. But it was a home in which she couldn't live.

CHAPTER 12

*S*ophie paced the office of the prime vizier. "But I have to go. You can't hold me here."

The prime vizier sighed. "Sophie, we've already been through this. His Royal Highness has forbidden you to leave until he returns from his travels around the country before the coronation. The contract you signed runs for another four months, but he's willing to forget the extra time. But you must fulfill your duties until coronation day."

"But why? Just tell me that."

The prime vizier frowned. "No. Now leave and continue with your work, as is required of you."

"What if I just leave?"

"You'll get nowhere. One call to airport security will ensure that. Now go. It's only for one more week."

Sophie could have screamed with frustration but couldn't say anything. How could she tell Mohammed that every minute she stayed in the palace, so close to Malek, but unable to have him as she wanted to, was painful beyond words for her? She had no alternative. "Okay. You have me for one more week. But I'd appreciate it if you could arrange my tickets, finalize my remuneration package, and ensure I have a driver at my disposal for a week today."

"Consider it done."

She walked quickly to her room and shut the door behind her. At least she could hide out in her suite of rooms. She'd been working from her room and no one had yet insisted she go to the office. She opened the doors that led to the courtyard, turned to her desk, and lost herself in the numbingly impersonal business of computer systems.

THE DAYS HAD DRAGGED from night to day, merging one into another. For the most part she stayed inside her bedroom, only emerging in the early hours and at dusk to stroll through the courtyards. Her food was brought to her without question, and she saw no one else.

But this was her final walk in the gardens she'd come to love, for Malek would return the next day and she couldn't risk bumping into him. She stepped outside into the fragrant evening and walked a little further, up to where the path emerged into a small area that overlooked the public spaces below.

She looked out at the lighthouse and remembered Malek telling her about his childhood. It seemed such a long time ago, not mere months. She remembered Queen Fairuza's words. Malek *had* changed, and Sophie had been partly responsible for that. She sighed. He was now a real part of his family's lives and she was on the outside, looking in. Just as she'd wanted. Wasn't it?

Suddenly voices rose from below. For one panicked moment she thought Malek had returned early. Then she listened more carefully and she could tell it wasn't him. The voice was very similar but the accent was different. He was speaking English with a vaguely antipodean accent. She frowned as she tried to place it.

Then the man's voice was joined by a woman's flirtatious giggle. The conversation between the man and the women was quick-paced and punctuated by laughter. Whoever they were, they were enjoying themselves.

Sophie's curiosity got the better of her, and she leaned over the stone balustrade and pushed away the bushes which obscured her view.

It *was* Malek! But then the man moved, and she saw his profile—equally strong, but more raw somehow, less handsome. It wasn't Malek. She breathed a deep sigh of relief and leaned against the balustrade for support. It must be one of the family—a cousin maybe—because the likeness was too close. But who was the woman?

She felt vaguely guilty peering over the balcony, watching them without their knowledge, but it was a public place, and they weren't in each other arms. It was just the tone of their voices which were flirtatious. She was too far away to hear exactly what they were saying.

The light was beginning to fade from the sky and the last of the sun's rays broke through a band of cloud that sat on the horizon, just at the same moment as the woman turned and leaned against a column. She lifted up her face to smile at the man and, with a jolt of shock, Sophie realized who the woman was. Flirting with a strange man, as if her life depended on it, was Sheikha Talisha—the woman who was at the top of the list to marry Malek!

Sophie stepped quietly from the balustrade. She'd seen enough. As she returned to her room, her mind raced. What would this mean for the future of the country? For Malek? If there was no marriage, then all their plans for peace could come to nothing, even with the queen's support. And if there was? Then Malek would marry someone who was obviously falling in love with another man.

~

THE MID-DAY SUN glinted off the gold flecks of the marble floor as Sophie paced her room. After seeing Sheikha Talisha two nights earlier, she'd spent over twenty-four hours trying to decide if she should tell Malek that the woman he was to marry was… what? Seen flirting with a man? It was hardly a hanging offense and Sophie knew it would make little difference to the outcome.

The marriage between Talisha and Malek was purely a business arrangement. Everyone, including the couple themselves, was clear on that point. But it made her heart ache to think of Malek tied to a loveless marriage. With her request for an audience refused because of an urgent all-day meeting, she'd finally written him a note. A note to which she'd received no reply. Nothing from Malek. Nothing from anyone. Even Raisa had deserted her. Her self-imposed exile seemed to suit the palace as it focused on catering for its swollen population and its preparations for the coronation.

And now it was the day of the coronation, and the key participants—including the Desert Kings—had been involved in meetings from dawn. It made Sophie uneasy, made her worry that something was amiss, but all the online news indicated everything was going to plan.

There was a knock at the door and Sophie started toward it, hoping beyond hope that Malek would be there. She opened it wide, but there was only the maid who had replaced Raisa.

"Where is Raisa?"

The girl smiled nervously and shrugged. "Very well."

Sophie sighed. The girl knew little English. There was no

point asking her if everything was going to plan. She missed Raisa—Raisa, who knew everything and who would have told her what, if anything, was going on. But, with the influx of visiting dignitaries into the palace Raisa's skills were in high demand and Sophie hadn't seen her in days.

The girl motioned for Sophie to sit before the mirror. As the girl switched on the hair straighteners and bustled around the small bathroom making sure she had everything ready to prepare Sophie for the afternoon ahead, Sophie glanced at her suitcase which was packed and ready for her departure that evening to Frankfurt. She could hardly believe she was leaving. But that was what she'd always wanted to do, wasn't it? To travel? To keep on moving?

She sat and faced the mirror while the girl worked her magic. Sophie had considered disobeying Prime Vizier Mohammed's instruction that she should attend the coronation, but it would be her last function. This time tomorrow, she'd be in Frankfurt. And, besides, there was a part of her which couldn't believe it—she needed to see with her own eyes that Malek truly was king, and was finally and completely unavailable to her.

SOPHIE STOOD outside a side door of the Great Hall. She should go in. She was dressed in her best evening gown, and had tried to prepare herself for this moment all week, but still she hesitated. The engagement and the coronation would happen at the same time. She simply couldn't do it.

She stepped away and sat on a seat close to the hall where she could hear the scatter of applause, the occasional cheer and the drone of the speaker. She'd listen to the ceremony from here and just imagine it.

She closed her eyes, and as the music struck up, she imagined Malek stepping forward onto the dais and the imam standing behind him, holding the crown aloft and intoning the age-old speech, before slowly placing the crown on his head.

The burst of simultaneous applause and music made her open her eyes. He must be king. She rose from the bench. The next bit of the ceremony she didn't want to imagine. She'd seen the order of ceremony and knew that, at this moment, his bride-to-be would come forward for the formal engagement.

Quickly she walked away from the hall toward the main fountain. The water splashed onto her ruby red satin gown, staining it like blood. "It's ruined," she whispered to herself and held up her hands to her eyes where the tears began to flow as freely as the water from the ornate stone fountain.

BY THE TIME she managed to find her way unaided across the palace grounds, avoiding the public thoroughfares, it was late. There was no one around. Everyone was at the coronation. She wondered if Malek would have the time or the interest to have looked for her at all. But even if he'd had the inclination, she knew he wouldn't have had the time. The sequence of events at the coronation was traditional and required the main players to be fully aware of what was going on at all times. One false move or word and the ceremony would have been brought into dishonor.

She opened her door and switched on the light. One look at the clock, and she realized she had no time to change. She'd have to go to the airport as she was and change there. She picked up the bags. They contained only what she'd brought into the country. All the best gowns she'd leave behind, save the one she was wearing. She had no wish to feel like she'd profited from this job in any other way than earning the salary which had been pre-arranged. She'd even returned the generous over-payment she'd discovered in her bank account.

No, she'd take what was hers, fair and square, and go to Frankfurt. And then… somewhere else.

She took one last look around the room that had been her home for the past few months, switched out the lights and closed the door behind her. The car would be waiting for her at the rear of the palace.

She trundled the cases around to the rear of the palace where, sure enough, a car was waiting for her. The palace was lit brightly by outside lights, and Sophie had to hold up her hand to ward off the glare to look inside. The driver was there.

A porter came forward and took her bags and put them in the trunk of the car. She was about to get in when Raisa came running out of the palace.

"Sophie! You weren't at the ceremony."

"I'm sorry, Raisa. But I couldn't go. I just couldn't."

There were tears in Raisa's eyes as Sophie embraced her. "So, you're leaving?"

"I have to. I'll keep in touch, I promise."

Raisa opened the door and Sophie got inside. Raisa closed it for her. She waved and, visibly upset, stepped away. "Goodbye," called Sophie as the car moved away from the palace.

Lost in her thoughts, Sophie let the tears flow unrestrained. Thoughts of Malek as she'd first seen him in Paris, striding through the hotel, authoritative and devastatingly handsome and sexy, then later in Sumaira, sitting watching her with an enigmatic smile on his face in business meetings, and then just a few days ago of Malek, naked, thrusting into her, bringing her to a climax. And now, she opened her eyes and watched the palace gates close behind them as they turned onto the highway that would take them to the airport.

She groped in her bag for a handkerchief and blew her nose. She couldn't let herself fall to pieces. She had her future to consider. She would cope. She *had* to cope. So, she'd done the last thing she'd wanted to do—she'd fallen in love. That meant only one thing... time to move on. Besides, even if Malek still wanted to marry her, there was no way his country would ever approve of the match. And there was no way that she could reveal the truth—that she loved him too much to destroy his tenuous peace with his mother and accept his proposal.

She closed her eyes and allowed herself the joy of thinking about Malek and of her time with him. She had five minutes before they reached the airport and she'd make the most of them.

But five minutes passed and they hadn't turned off the highway. She opened her eyes with a start and didn't recognize where they were. She looked behind her and saw the telltale shape of the hangars receding into the dark.

She leaned forward. "We've missed the turn off to the airport. It was back there."

The driver didn't answer but took the next turning off the highway in the opposite direction. The track was rough, and panic grew in Sophie as she realized they were heading toward the sea. In front of her was the lighthouse that could be seen from the palace, the one Malek had told her about. What the hell was going on?

"The airport is the other way," she repeated, trying to sound firm rather than frightened.

The man said nothing but swung the car around in front of the lighthouse. "I know," a familiar voice said. "But don't worry, you won't miss your flight, *if* you still wish to go."

That voice. *That* voice. Stunned, Sophie froze while the driver got out and came around and opened her door. Speechless, she sat looking up at the man who, she realized now, wasn't dressed in palace livery, but an expensive designer suit. Silhouetted against the lighter sky, she couldn't see the man's features but she recognized *that* voice. "Sophie, I want to show you something."

His hand stretched out to her and trembling, she raised hers and he grasped it and pulled her out of the car.

"Malek?" She reached up her hand to his face, her hand shaking until she pressed it against his cheek. "Is it really you?"

She felt his smile form under her palm. "Yes."

"But what the hell are you doing here?"

"I needed to see you, to tell you what this all means for us."

"What are you talking about?"

"Do you truly not know? Haven't you heard what happened?"

She shook her head, completely confused.

"Then, my love, I will tell you as we walk." He took her hand. "Come."

Sophie wondered if she were dreaming. There was nothing but darkness all around them—punctuated only by the flash from the lighthouse in which she caught Malek's cheek in profile one moment, his devastating smile the next —as they walked along the rocky path to the cliff edge. Before them, the midnight blue sea stretched like a swathe of rumpled velvet, occasionally pricked by the white of water splashing on the rocks below, and traces of phosphorescence.

He looked up at the lighthouse. "Do you remember me telling you about the lighthouse? How I used to watch the regular flash of light. How it was always there. I found comfort in the steady rhythm, despite this turbulent land and family of mine."

"But shouldn't you be with your family now? Malek, what

the hell is going on? What about your fiancée, your country, the celebrations... You should *be* there."

"No, I shouldn't. I couldn't tell you; there wasn't time. But everything has changed. I revoked my constitutional rights in favor of my brother."

"Your brother? But he's—" She stopped as she suddenly remembered the man's faint Australian accent in the court-yard below her the previous night. "He's here? In Sumaira?"

"Apparently my mother decided it would be in everyone's best interests if he became king in my place."

"She did *what?*"

"So she contacted him and persuaded him to return and take up the throne. It seems he didn't need much persuading, especially when he realized Sheikha Talisha would be his fiancée. You were right about Talisha having met Jaish at Oxford. Seems they did a little more than meet, but couldn't take it any further as she'd been off-limits during my father's reign."

"And all this is acceptable to your government, your people, to your country? This switch at the last minute?"

"My country is very different to any Western country. Our royal family *is* the government, essentially. Besides, all the principal tribes agree. Jaish has been groomed to be king from birth. To them it doesn't matter if it's one brother or the other." He shrugged. "We swapped places, had the changes ratified by government and Jaish has now been crowned King of Sumaira and is engaged to the sheikha. And, is, as far as I can see, very happy about it all."

"Then why did he leave in the first place?" Sophie felt angry on Malek's behalf. "Your brother put you through all of this when he was happy to be king in the first place?"

"He's been away in Australia a year and that time has changed him. He'd grown up under the spotlight, and I think he needed time away to think things through. He was deep in the Outback when my mother tracked him down. It was only because his horse had gone lame and he'd had to return to the station that she managed to speak with him. It seems he'd come to something of a turning point and was ready to return. He had no idea of the state of things here, or else I think he'd have returned sooner." He sighed. "Anyway, he's home, he's king, and that leaves me…" He grinned as he turned to Sophie and took her hand. "Free."

"Free to do?"

He brought her hand to his lips and kissed it. "Exactly as I like."

"And what do you like?"

"I'd like to escape Sumaira—at least for a while—and return either to Paris or London or maybe somewhere else. Just… be free."

"And then?"

"I'll continue the work I've begun here, to make Sumaira great again. I'll move between countries negotiating trade deals which will see our ports busy, and our men employed once more."

"Always on the move."

"That depends."

"On?" The small syllable hung in the air. Sophie could have sworn the thud of her heart was audible.

"On what my wife wishes to do. You see, I'm back to square one. I need to find a wife."

She felt a sob rise which she tried to prevent from surfacing but failed. He took her hands in both of his and caressed them. "Don't you understand?" His eyes flashed hot and intense under the intermittent flash. Instead of warming her, it provoked another sob to rise in her throat. She kept her lips pressed tight together to prevent them from shaking. She shook her head.

"Then I'll have to make it plain. You found the future

Queen of Sumaira, but you've yet to keep your end of the bargain and find *me* someone to marry."

She sucked in another difficult breath. "That's not plain."

"My list contained everything I believed, and that I'd been told, was required of a wife." He shook his head, his fingers sweeping over her hands. "But it wasn't complete. I couldn't know what I needed when I wrote that list. Because I hadn't met you."

The strength suddenly left Sophie's body, and he pulled her into his arms.

He lifted her face to his, cradling it in his hands. "*You*, Sophie." He searched her face. "I can't make a list of things. I can't separate out the things which make me want you, need you, love you. Sophie, *habibti*, I want to begin my new life by repeating a question I posed a week ago."

"My answer, then, you know, I couldn't—"

"Sophie, it's okay. I know what happened. My mother told me everything. I know now I asked you a question you couldn't answer in the affirmative without going back on your word to my mother. She told me everything."

"Oh." Sophie exhaled softly, the tension draining from her. "Thank goodness. But..." She trailed off as tears overwhelmed her.

"I know you, Sophie. I know you're scared of love and commitment—of being hurt—scared of being lost, as your mother was. But life without love isn't worth living. I can vouch for that because I've spent half my life like that. You've shown me a different way. Now, it's *my* turn to show *you*. Because I love you and I'll always make sure you're safe. You'll never be lost, never hurt, with me."

The tears only increased as she instinctively recognized the truth in his words. She tried to swipe the tears from her face, but he stopped her and swept his thumbs across her cheeks and held her face in his hands.

"Sophie, marry me, please."

Her tears flowed over his fingers and all she could do was nod.

His eyes lit up under the flash of the lighthouse. "Is that a 'yes'?"

She nodded again, unable to speak—her heart was too full. Then she gasped in a lungful of air. "It's a complete and utter 'yes,'" she managed to whisper before his lips claimed hers in a kiss which she never wanted to end.

EPILOGUE

Six months later...

"Are you okay?" whispered a concerned Malek to Sophie as they stepped out of his grandmother's apartment in the palace, where they lived when they were in Sumaira. "The heat is not too much for you after the cold of Paris?"

"Malek! You worry too much. I'm only pregnant. I can cope with a bit of heat."

"Pregnant with *twins*." His hand briefly caressed her five-month bump.

"And never been healthier. So stop worrying and take me to your leader." She grinned.

He gave her an answering smile and put his arm casually around her waist. She knew what he was doing. Just as he always did, supporting her without drawing attention to the fact.

"Come, the family is in the anteroom; we'll join them there before we proceed into the Great Hall for the ceremony."

Sophie and Malek were soon swallowed up by his noisy, talkative family who had all rallied behind the new king to present a united front to the world. Today was the day when a new treaty would be signed between the Desert Kings and the countries to the east which had threatened Sumaira in recent years. Now, the Desert Kings were all able to move forward toward a more peaceful era.

They walked into the Great Hall in one long line, Malek to the right of his brother, the King of Sumaira, and Sophie to his right. The king's new wife was to his left and to her left, Queen Mother Fairuza and Prime Vizier Mohammed, who were now engaged to be married. Behind them were numerous cousins and family who'd made the journey from all over Sumaira and overseas to be there on this momentous day.

After initial greetings, Malek insisted a chair be brought for Sophie, much to her chagrin. But sometimes, thought Sophie, as she did as she was told, the remnants of Malek's autocratic kingly air were overwhelmingly sexy. Besides, being seated gave her the opportunity to observe the Desert Kings and their families—Kings Zahir, Razeen and Tariq, and Princes Sahmir and Daidan. The feeling today was quite different to eight months ago. Now there was a feeling of optimism in the air. Only King Tariq of the Desert Kings was married with children. Although rumor had it that he wasn't happily so. His wife appeared to spend more time abroad than in his country.

Sophie shifted her gaze from Tariq and Zahir—both imposing and solemn men—to the others, who were younger and single.

There would be many changes afoot in the lands of the Desert Kings in the years to come. Changes she and Malek would witness as they moved between countries, working for continued peace and increasing prosperity in their world.

Suddenly everyone rose, and she looked around in surprise. She must have been lost in her thoughts as it seemed the formal part of the meeting was over and people moved around, greeting old friends and allies.

Malek rose and held out his hand to help her up. She might be only five months pregnant, but with twins she looked as though she were nearly full term. He inclined his head to hers. "You are so beautiful, *habibti*, all I could think of, all through the ceremony, was you lying naked on our bed this morning, your legs wide open for me."

She half-laughed, half-coughed in surprise at the inappropriate remark. "It was too hot to be covered with a sheet."

"Even if it weren't, I would have pulled it off you because, my darling, I can't get enough of you."

She became instantly wet as she remembered his mouth on her sex only hours earlier, giving her what she wanted, bringing her to the ecstatic climax which grew only more rewarding and richer with time.

She leaned her head against his shoulder. "If you don't want me to either have an orgasm on the spot or faint through overheating, you'd better stop talking like that."

"Hm." He narrowed his eyes sexily. "I'll tell Jaish that we have to leave. I'll tell him that my wife is demanding sex, and I must satisfy her."

"No!" She laughed but he stepped away.

"Wait by the door for me. It's cooler there. I won't be long, and I will give you what you want. It's the least I can do. After all, you did find me a wife."

Sophie watched with a grin as Malek spoke with Jaish, about what she didn't know. She just hoped he was only teasing her and not telling his brother the truth. But then his brother grinned and clapped Malek on the back and raised an eyebrow at her and she shook her head and looked away in embarrassment.

"Ready?" Malek asked.

"Always, my love."

They stepped outside into a future as bright as the sunlight.

King Zahir of Qawaran watched Malek and Sophie walk out the room, so close, so happy, then turned his attention to the rest of the Sumairan royal family, marveling at the difference six months could make. At the Desert Kings summit held in Paris eight months earlier, he'd willingly pledged his allegiance to the group, even if he had been doubtful as to the future of Sumaira. Loyalty and duty to family and friends meant everything to Zahir. As far as he was concerned, there was nothing else.

The thought of disloyalty brought a bitter taste of bile to his mouth, as did his memory of that meeting in Paris. It had been there that he'd met Anna, the woman with whom he'd had a love affair which was as dramatic as it had been brief. One night of intense lovemaking and then… it had ended as suddenly as it had begun.

"Lost in thought, Zahir?" He greeted Razeen, who'd recently become King of Sitra after the sudden death of his father and brother.

"Remembering Paris."

"Yes, we've all come a long way since then. Who would have believed Malek and Jaish could have created the foundations of a strong and prosperous country so quickly."

"There's still a lot of work to do."

"Yes, but they've a sound base from which grow. We couldn't have foreseen that eight months ago."

We couldn't have foreseen a lot of things, Zahir thought. Least of all that the woman he'd fallen for had turned out to be married to his brother; had turned out to be a disloyal, adulterous liar, with whom he was still completely obsessed.

"Just goes to show that one never knows what may happen in the future. What can appear impossible one day, can be happening the next," said Razeen.

Zahir looked out the window toward the distant line of mountains that separated his land-locked country from Sumaira and wondered if Razeen just might be right.

AFTERWORD

Thank you for reading *Wanted: A Wife for the Sheikh*. I hope you enjoyed it! Reviews are always welcome—they help me, and they help prospective readers to decide if they'd enjoy the book.

Although this book was written after the others, it's a prequel to the series and introduces the Kings and Princes of Desert Kings fame who feature in the other five books in the series:

Wanted: A Wife for the Sheikh
The Sheikh's Bargain Bride
The Sheikh's Lost Lover
Awakened by the Sheikh
Claimed by the Sheikh
Wanted: A Baby by the Sheikh

If you'd like to find out if Razeen is right about the future and whether Zahir's future isn't as gloomy as he predicts, pick up a copy of *The Sheikh's Bargain Bride* today (excerpt follows). Here's a review of *The Sheikh's Bargain Bride* to give you a taste of what to expect.

"This story easily swept me off my feet and tumbled me around a little before setting me down gently. Exotic locations, exotic characters, love, revenge, secrets, and heartache all come together perfectly to create an emotional yet romantic tale." (MsRomanticReads)

For more information about my books and to sign up to my newsletter, please check out my website: www.dianafraser.com.

Happy reading!

Diana

～

THE SHEIKH'S BARGAIN BRIDE

BOOK 2 OF DESERT KINGS—ZAHIR

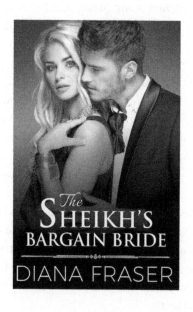

Anna Whitman has yearned for freedom and independence her whole life but she's forced to accept a marriage of convenience so she can live with her son.

Sheikh Zahir Al-Zaman is a ruthless desert warrior who believes the only way he can control his obsession with Anna is to possess her. And he'll do almost anything—even kidnap her son—to have her.

But Zahir will not force her into his bed. He has his strategies for seduction—strategies Anna finds increasingly hard to resist. But she won't have a relationship based on lies. And how can she reveal her secrets when they will shatter the beliefs he holds most dear?

Excerpt

Sheikh Zahir al-Zaman narrowed his eyes against the glare of the sun-bleached stony plains and focused on the slowly materializing dark speck. Within minutes the helicopter's low rhythmic thrum filled the overcast spring sky like an angry locust intent on devastation.

She hadn't wasted any time. But then he'd made sure she couldn't refuse his invitation. He banished a flicker of discomfort with practiced ease. Sometimes you had to lure the prey to you. Sometimes, in a way that wasn't palatable.

But the ends always justified the means. She *would* be his and he was prepared to do whatever it took to make it happen.

He watched the helicopter alight in a cloud of dust before the palace. The pilot lifted out a small case and began to open the door before it was pushed open abruptly from within and two long, jean-clad legs emerged. A tall blonde jumped down and looked around the palace, her head twisting and turning impatiently.

She'd changed. She was thinner, her hair longer, her face no longer sun-kissed but as pale as the desert under moonlight. Still, his body responded the same to her now, as it did when she visited him in his dreams.

He'd lived with his obsession with her for six long years: cursing and nurturing the anger at her deceit and betrayal while still longing to relive the passion of their one night together. But his brother's death meant he no longer had to live with the madness.

Then, with an imperceptible movement of her head, she looked up and saw him. Zahir frowned and his breath caught unexpectedly in his chest. Ice blue eyes stared at him, challenging him, demanding an explanation from him. How could eyes so cool and northern spark such fire? She turned away suddenly and slid the door of the helicopter shut with a force that belied her fragility. The metallic crash echoed around the palace, destroying its peace and order.

He'd get what he wanted but he knew, without a doubt, that it wasn't going to be easy.

Buy Now!

~

Made in the USA
Las Vegas, NV
08 April 2022

47061322R00108